Trial
–by–
Poison

Trailblazer Books

TITLE	HISTORIC CHARACTERS
Attack in the Rye Grass	Marcus & Narcissa Whitman
The Bandit of Ashley Downs	George Müller
The Chimney Sweep's Ransom	John Wesley
Escape from the Slave Traders	David Livingstone
The Hidden Jewel	Amy Carmichael
Imprisoned in the Golden City	Adoniram and Ann Judson
Kidnapped by River Rats	William & Catherine Booth
Listen for the Whippoorwill	Harriet Tubman
The Queen's Smuggler	William Tyndale
Shanghaied to China	Hudson Taylor
Spy for the Night Riders	Doctor Martin Luther
Trial by Poison	Mary Slessor

Trial
—by—
Poison

DAVE & NETA JACKSON

Text Illustrations by
Julian Jackson

BETHANY HOUSE PUBLISHERS
MINNEAPOLIS, MINNESOTA 55438

Inside illustrations by Julian Jackson
Cover design and illustration by Catherine Reishus McLaughlin

Published by Bethany House Publishers
A Ministry of Bethany Fellowship, Inc.
11300 Hampshire Avenue South
Minneapolis, Minnesota 55438

Printed in the United States of America

Library of Congress Cataloging-in-Publication Data

Jackson, Dave.
    Trial by poison / Dave Jackson, Neta Jackson.
        p.   cm. — (Trailblazer books)
    Includes bibliographical references.
    Summary: In 1888, change arrives in a small village in Calabar,
Nigeria in the form of a courageous missionary named Mary.

    1. Slessor, Mary Mitchell, 1848–1915—Juvenile fiction.
    [1. Slessor, Mary Mitchell, 1848–1915—Fiction.
2. Missionaries—Fiction. 3. Nigeria—Fiction.] I. Jackson,
Neta. II. Title. III. Series.
PZ7.J132418Tr   1994
[Fic]—dc20   94–7587
ISBN 1–55661–274–5   CIP
                                          AC

The main characters and major events in this story are true. However, certain events (such as the trading expedition and Etim's accident) do not follow the actual timeline. In the same way, certain minor historical characters have been left out of the narrative to simplify the story. In particular:

The woman named Inyam was indeed a relative by marriage to Chief Edem, and her teenage daughter (whom we have named Imatu) was a cousin of Etim, the chief's son. The real names of Mary's two foster sons (whom we call Okot and Udo) are not known.

The incident of Imatu breaking a taboo by entering the boys' yard is based on an actual incident in another village in which two sixteen-year-old harem wives entered the boys' yard on a lark, and would have been given a hundred lashes if Mary Slessor had not intervened.

We have merged the incident of finding the baby in the bush with the events surrounding Etim's funeral; it actually took place later, and the child was "heard" by village women on their way to market.

Finally, the time frame for the first communion service, which actually took place on Mary Slessor's fifteenth anniversary in Okoyong, was shortened by about half for the purposes of our story. Also the story tells only about one set of baptisms; the next day eleven younger children were also baptized, among them six of Mary's adopted children.

DAVE AND NETA JACKSON are a husband/wife writing team who have authored or coauthored many books on marriage and family, the church, and relationships, including the books accompanying the Secret Adventures video series, the Pet Parables series, and the Caring Parent series.

They have three children: Julian, the illustrator for the Trailblazer series, Rachel, a college student, and Samantha, their high school Cambodian foster daughter. They make their home in Evanston, Illinois, where they are active members of Reba Place Church.

CONTENTS

Chapter 1

The White Ma and the Royal Canoe

PRESSING HER BODY against a twisted mangrove tree, Imatu peered around the trunk. There. She could see the goat a short distance away, flicking its tail and munching the grass along the riverbank.

I'll catch you now, Imatu thought grimly. A light rain was falling steadily through the forest, covering any noise she might make.

But before Imatu could move, the goat threw its head up, gave a startled leap, and disappeared into the wet, dripping bushes.

"Wicked goat!" Imatu fumed, stamping her foot in frustration.

She had been trying to catch the runaway since noon and had followed it all the way to the Calabar River. At first she'd been glad her mother had sent her after the missing goat—that meant she didn't have to go to the funeral in Ifako, the next village. Imatu hated funerals. All the drinking made everyone crazy, and the witch doctor was sure to accuse someone of casting a spell on the person who had died.

But the light was slipping away in the late, rainy afternoon, and Imatu didn't want to be in the forest after dark. She'd been so close to catching that goat! She knew she hadn't made any noise. What had startled it?

Then she heard it. Chanting . . . coming from the river.

The chanting grew louder, accompanied by the steady swish, swish of paddles dipping into the water. Who was coming up the river? Imatu's heart beat faster; she was tempted to turn and run back to the village. But curiosity moved her feet quietly through the wet grass, stepping over gnarled tree roots and tangled vines, toward the edge of the river.

The girl crouched behind a bush and listened. She could make out some of the words now . . .

Ma, our beautiful, beloved mother,
Is on board.
Ho! Ho! Ho!

And then the canoe came in sight. Imatu gasped. She had never seen a canoe like this one! It was twice as long as the fishing canoes the men of her village hollowed out of fallen tree trunks. From front to back, strong paddlers lined either side—more than she could count!—their dark skin glistening in the rain. A steersman stood in the back, beside a pole with a long banner flying out behind. But strangest of all was the little "hut" in the middle of the canoe, covered on top by palm leaves, with brightly colored cloth curtains fluttering on all sides.

The canoe shot past her, on up the river. Imatu ran after it, safely hidden among the bushes and trees of the forest. This was no fishing canoe. It couldn't belong to an ordinary village chief. This must be a *king's* canoe.

Whump! A hidden tree root sent Imatu sprawling on the ground. She scrambled to her feet but she could no longer see the canoe, though she could still hear the chanting . . . *Ho! Ho! Ho!* Ignoring her stinging toes and knees, Imatu ran faster. She had never seen a king before—the Okoyong people had no king. So where did this king come from? And where was he going?

Suddenly the chanting stopped. Coming over a little rise beside the river, Imatu quickly crouched down. The canoe had pulled up onto a little strip of sand. The front paddlers hopped out and pulled the canoe halfway out of the water and started to unload bags and boxes. But Imatu's eyes were riveted on the little hut.

The curtains parted and a young boy and girl crawled out. Right behind them, an older boy about

Imatu's age came out, holding a small child on his hip. The children scrambled over the side of the big canoe, squealing, obviously glad to stretch their legs after being cooped up in the little hut.

But where was the king?

The curtains parted again and a woman came out, holding a baby. Imatu shook the rain out of her eyes; the fading light must be playing tricks on her! She squeezed her eyes shut, then opened them and stared again.

The woman's skin had no color! It was as white as the goat Imatu had been chasing all afternoon. And her hair! It was reddish orange—as orange as the yams Imatu and her mother dug out of the ground to roast and eat.

Imatu had never seen a white person before. What was a white woman doing in a king's canoe? Imatu's heart thudded so loudly in her chest she was afraid the people from the canoe could hear it, too. Had this strange woman brought warriors to attack her village while everyone was away at the funeral? Everyone, that is, except Imatu's mother and a few slave women. . . .

Just then the strange white woman called out to the oldest boy: "Okin! Gather the children and follow that path." Imatu was startled; the woman was speaking in Efik, her own language! "And, Akani," the woman said to the steersman, "the children and I are going ahead. You organize the bearers and bring the supplies. We need to get to Ekenge before dark . . . about four miles into the forest."

Ekenge! That was Imatu's village. The white woman *was* going there!

Imatu jumped quietly to her feet, still careful not to be seen, and ran as fast as she could through the tangled underbrush toward her village. When she thought she was well ahead of the strangers, she found the path that led from the river to the village. The rain had slowed to a drizzle, but the path was wet and slippery.

Daylight was almost gone when Imatu stumbled into the nearly deserted village. Ekenge, like other Okoyong villages, was a loose cluster of family compounds. Each compound consisted of several huts grouped together behind a rough bamboo fence for a man, his wives, their children, several slaves, and assorted animals. Tonight the compound fires were cold—except for one.

Slipping in the mud, Imatu made her way toward the single fire flickering in the drizzling rain. Her mother, Inyam, was stirring a mush made of corn-meal under a palm-thatch shelter, while two old women—slaves of the chief—sat in the doorway of one of the huts.

"Mem! Mem!" Imatu called out, gasping from her run.

"Imatu? Did you find the goat?" her mother called back. Inyam was a handsome woman, large boned and strong.

"No . . . the goat . . . not important . . . woman coming . . ." gasped Imatu.

"What?" said Inyam angrily. "You came back

14

without the goat? Go! Go now and find it, or the chief will beat us when he returns."

"Wait! Wait!" pleaded Imatu. "I came to warn you . . . a woman with many warriors . . . coming!"

"Woman? What woman?" frowned her mother.

"A *white* woman! In a king's canoe!"

Inyam grabbed Imatu by the shoulders and gave her a shake. "You're talking crazy! Who gave you gin to drink?"

Suddenly they heard the sound of children crying, coming from the forest path. Imatu's mother stared in astonishment as the white woman with short, red hair marched barefoot and hatless out of the brush and into the muddy clearing, carrying a year-old infant. Clinging to her skirts were two children crying lustily. Imatu saw that the boy called Okin was right on her heels, carrying another whimpering child.

The two old slave women gave a fearful cry and scurried into the hut. But Inyam walked slowly toward the pathetic little group standing in the middle of the village. Imatu crowded close behind her, peeking around her mother's back.

"Oh! I'm so glad to see you!" said the stranger, shifting the baby to her other hip. "I'm looking for Chief Edem, village of Ekenge."

Inyam looked the woman up and down. "You have warriors?" she asked.

"Warriors? No, no," the woman shook her head, trying vainly to shush the tired, wet children. "I come as a friend. I am a Jesus teacher."

Inyam frowned at the strange name. "Jesus teacher? Is he the king of the canoe?"

"The king of the . . . what?" Then the woman laughed. "Oh, the canoe! No, no. The canoe belongs to my friend, King Eyo Honesty VII of Creek Town. The king loaned me his canoe because I had no way to come up the river—"

Just then a man ran out from the forest path into the village clearing. Inyam tensed; Imatu recognized him as the steersman of the canoe.

"Ma! Ma Slessor!" the man cried, panting from his run. "The paddlers will not bring your supplies tonight. They say it is too dark; they are afraid of the evil spirits in the forest. They will come tomorrow."

For a moment the white woman's shoulders seemed to sag. Then she lifted her head. "No, tomorrow is Sunday, God's day of rest. I cannot ask them to work for me tomorrow. It must be tonight. Here," she said to a startled Inyam, handing the baby to Imatu's mother. "Will you please take care of my children until I get back? It seems I must go shake the men myself. Come, Akani." And with that the woman plunged back into the now-dark forest, the steersman at her heels.

Inyam just stared after her, openmouthed, the baby screaming in her arms. Imatu tugged at her mother's skirt and pointed to the pot of cornmeal mush still cooking on the sputtering fire. "We can feed them," she suggested, suddenly feeling sorry for the children, who had just been abandoned by their "mother" . . . or whoever that white woman was.

In a short while the five children were greedily stuffing cornmeal mush into their mouths and being fussed over by the two old slave women who had come out when the white woman left.

"No milk to drink," Imatu said, shrugging her shoulders at the boy named Okin. "I lost the goat."

Imatu woke with a start. The rain had stopped, the baby was asleep in Inyam's arms, and the white woman's other children had curled up on mats inside the hut. But she saw the dancing light of many torches approaching the village and heard drums beating and drunken singing. Was it the white woman returning? . . . No, the torches were coming from the direction of Ifako. The villagers must be returning from the funeral.

Inyam had heard the commotion, too, and was trying to lay the baby down without waking it up when a tall man in a flowing robe strode toward their still flickering fire.

"Inyam!" he bellowed angrily. "Why did you not go to the funeral? You dishonor me and our sister village by your absence!"

Imatu's mother scrambled to her feet, her eyes cast down. "I didn't mean to dishonor you, brother-in-law," she said. "The goat that my dead husband left us—it ran away. Imatu and I had to find it, so that we do not presume further on your generous hospitality."

"A likely story!" roared the man, who was obviously drunk. "You probably untied it yourself to have an excuse not to go to the funeral, you insolent woman! And . . . what is this baby? Whose orphan did you snatch from the forest? Do you think our poor village can feed another mouth? I won't have it! I—"

"Chief Edem!"

A powerful woman's voice carried through the night, over the babble of voices slurred with strong drink. All eyes turned in the direction of the path that led to the river, and voices suddenly ceased. Into the circle of torchlight marched the white woman with red hair, followed by a line of unhappy-looking men carrying all sorts of boxes and bundles.

"Chief Edem," said the woman again in the Efik language, addressing Inyam's brother-in-law. "The baby is my adopted child. I am Mary Slessor; do you remember me? You and I talked in a big *palaver* once before, almost two years ago, and you invited me to come to your village and teach 'book.' Well, I am here."

The drunken chief's eyes bugged and his mouth opened and shut, but no sound came out. Imatu felt like giggling but dared not. And then in the silence she heard a forlorn "baaaa."

Attached to Mary Slessor's wrist was a braided vine, and at the other end of the vine was the missing goat.

Chapter 2

"Run, Ma! Run!"

CHIEF EDEM WAS SO ASTONISHED to see Mary Slessor that he forgot his anger at Inyam and Imatu. He said no more about the runaway goat, which Imatu tied up next to her mother's hut. The drunken chief merely stalked away, and Mary and the canoe men were left to sleep among her boxes and bundles as best they could.

Early the next morning, the red-haired woman fed the canoe paddlers from her supplies, then sent them off to return King Eyo's canoe. While the chief and most of the people were sleeping off the effects of their drinking binge at the funeral,

Imatu saw the Jesus teacher do a strange thing: She covered one of her boxes with a pretty cloth on which she laid a book and a bouquet of purple orchids and yellow jasmine picked from the edge of the forest. Then she started talking to the handful of children and slave women who had gathered around curiously.

"This book is called the Bible," explained Mary. "It is God's Word to *all* people—white people like me and black people like you. It tells the story of God the Father, who loves you. In fact, He sent His Son Jesus to take the punishment for all of our sins. Today is Sunday, the first day of the week, a day God set aside for us to worship Him and thank Him for His love."

She was speaking in the Efik language, but the words were very strange to Imatu. Whatever was she talking about? The only gods Imatu knew about were angry spirits, putting curses and spells on people and requiring blood sacrifice to satisfy their anger. Imatu was afraid of gods, and she didn't trust this new one, either. But she liked the woman's gentle smile as she spoke.

Imatu milked the goat and brought the milk in a clay bowl for Mary's children to drink, along with some boiled yams and rice that her mother had cooked. The strange family had set up "camp" among their boxes and bundles, and Imatu squatted nearby, watching as they ate. Then, shyly, she pointed at each of the children in turn and looked quizzically at Mary.

Mary smiled and nodded. "This is Annie," she said, giving the baby a playful shake. Then she tapped the two younger boys, who had cooked yam smeared on their faces. "Okot is three years old and Udo is eight. Janie . . ." Mary gave the little girl, who was about six years old, a big hug. "Janie has been my own sweet adopted daughter since she was a baby, just like Annie. And then there is Okin . . ."

The older boy looked embarrassed.

"Okin is on loan to me," Mary went on, "because his mother wants him to be trained in God's ways. I couldn't manage without Okin—he's the man in our family, even though he is just eleven."

"I am twelve," Imatu spoke up proudly. "My father died last year—that's why my mother and I live in my uncle's compound. But my uncle doesn't . . ."

Imatu's voice trailed off and her eyes widened with alarm. A sober Chief Edem was approaching the little group, accompanied by a very large woman and a boy about sixteen. The three of them were wearing their best clothes, and the boy had a drum slung over his shoulder on a snakeskin strap.

Had her uncle heard her?

But Chief Edem ignored Imatu and spoke to his guest. "We welcome you, Ma Slessor!" he boomed, as if she had just arrived. "This is Etim, my oldest son, who will be chief after me. And this is my sister, Eme Ete. She will show you a hut for you and your children in the women's yard of my own compound. You are our honored guest."

Mary Slessor thanked the chief warmly and fol-

lowed his very large sister into the chief's compound as Etim beat importantly on his drum. Now that the chief had officially welcomed the white woman, all the other villagers crowded in, too, not wanting to miss anything that this strange person might do. The children pinched her skin to see if it was the same as theirs; the women touched her straight red hair and laughed. But "Ma Slessor" just smiled and laughed along with them as she dragged her boxes and bundles behind the chief's bamboo fence.

The next morning Imatu woke up to discover Ma Slessor and an amused Eme Ete—whom everyone called "Ma Eme"—vigorously sweeping out the filthy hut with palm branches, repairing the sagging roof with fresh palms, and hanging a curtain of cloth in the doorway. The boxes and bundles all went inside the hut—though at night, they all had to come out again, so that the white Ma and her children could sleep inside.

Imatu left the frenzied cleaning and took the four goats from Chief Edem's compound into the forest in search of sweet grass to eat—her daily job. Today she kept the braided vine around the neck of her mother's goat to make sure it didn't run away. When she returned in midafternoon, Ma Slessor was talking to her mother and several "lesser" wives and slave women of the chief.

" . . . to learn to read 'book,' " the white woman was saying.

"But we are women," Inyam protested. "Surely the chief will not let us."

23

"And we are slaves," several other women snorted bitterly.

"It doesn't matter," Ma Slessor insisted. "I talked *palaver* with the chief. If one person learns to read, all must be able to learn to read, whether chief or slave, man or woman or child. That is my rule."

Sure enough, a curious crowd of about thirty men, women, and children, both slave and free, gathered around the missionary in the village clearing for their first reading lesson. Ma Slessor held up a slate with a funny mark on it and made a sound. Everyone repeated the sound. Then she turned the slate over and scratched a new funny mark on the other side and made a different sound. Everyone repeated the second sound. Back and forth they went between the two marks, each representing its own sound.

"She is teaching the Efik alphabet," Okin whispered to Imatu.

Imatu was excited. Would she really be able to learn "book"? Just then she glanced up and saw her cousin Etim, the chief's son, standing off to the side with his drum, smirking. He didn't say anything, but she could read his sneer: *Huh! Reading is for slave women and children. You won't catch the chief's son doing such a "womanish" thing.*

Imatu looked away. She didn't care what stupid old Etim thought.

Reading School was held in the early evening after the slave men and women got back from tending their masters' or mistresses' "farms"—plots of land scattered in forest clearings where each extended family grew yams and cassava roots, red peppers and corn, beans and rice. The children in each compound milked the goats and fed the scrawny chickens that provided eggs and sometimes meat to flavor a pot of vegetables. Men and boys also went fishing in the Calabar River to supplement the meager food supply.

Ma Eme still had a farm near her old village, where she had lived with her husband before she became a widow. Several days after Ma Slessor arrived, when the August rains had slowed a little bit, the chief's sister announced that she was going to the farm to check on one of her slave women, who was pregnant and about to have a baby. Ma Slessor politely asked if she could go along. Ma Eme was pleased, and together with baby Annie and Ma Slessor's three boys, they set off.

But six-year-old Janie had stepped on a thorn and couldn't walk such a distance, so Imatu quickly volunteered to take care of her. The older girl carried the younger girl on her back, following the goats to a nearby clearing, where the rainy season had created a carpet of rich grass. As noontime came and went, the goats lay in patches of welcome sunshine, chewing their cud.

"Where's your *real* mother, Janie?" Imatu asked, weaving tiny orchids into the little girl's hair.

The little girl looked confused. "Ma is my mother," she said.

"But she's a white woman. Her people must live across the sea."

Janie brightened. "Oh, yes. Ma is from Scotland. It's cold and rainy there, and all the houses are made from wood and stones, all crowded together in a big city. . . ."

Imatu's eyes widened. "How do you know?"

Janie's white teeth flashed a big smile in her pretty, dark face. "She took me there when I was a baby. I wore English dresses and learned to talk English, too. And we had tea and biscuits every morning for breakfast. I don't remember going there—but I do remember coming back to Calabar on a great big ship across the ocean."

Imatu thought about this. She could hardly believe that little Janie had been on a big ship, bigger than the king's canoe, and had gone across the ocean to a country named Scotland full of pale people with red hair.

"But where's your *Calabar* mother and father?" she finally asked.

Janie shrugged. "I don't know. They didn't want me, I guess. But Ma did."

Then the little girl, her head crowned with a wreath of little orchids, looked curiously at her new friend. "Your mother lives in Chief Edem's compound like his other wives. Is Chief Edem your father?"

Imatu scowled. "No, he's my uncle. . . . Never mind. It's time to take the goats back to the village."

After that day, Janie Slessor often begged to be allowed to go with Imatu to take care of the goats. Imatu didn't mind; it was like having a little sister to play with and talk to. She had felt very lonely ever since she and her mother had moved away from their own village a few months ago. For some reason the other children in Ekenge seemed to ignore her when they were playing games or telling secrets. But now Okin and his "brothers" and "sisters" were her friends, which raised her status in the eyes of the other village children.

Even though Okin was a year younger than she was, Imatu was impressed at his friendliness and helpfulness toward everyone—not like her cousin Etim, who was always playing his stupid drum and would barely speak to Imatu. And Okin was a good worker, just like Ma Slessor had said. Even Ma Eme decided to send him on an errand to her farm one day because she was feeling "poorly" and didn't want to make the trip.

That evening as Reading School began, Okin still wasn't back from Ma Eme's farm. Imatu was disappointed because Okin had been helping her review the alphabet sounds she had learned. This evening, Imatu was struggling by herself with two new alphabet sounds when she thought she heard someone shouting in the forest. A moment later, Okin came running out of the trees, calling frantically, "Run, Ma, run!"

Dropping her slate, Ma Slessor ran to meet him, followed by half the Reading School.

"The babies . . . the babies . . ." he gasped.

The crowd around Okin parted as Ma Eme shouldered her way to the boy. "Is it my slave woman? Did she have her baby? What has happened?" the big woman demanded.

Okin looked frightened and turned toward Ma Slessor. "It's . . . it's twins. You have to run, Ma, or they will kill them!"

Ma Eme let out a roar. "Twins! That evil woman! She has been dancing with the devil and pretending all is well. And after I have treated her like my own daughter . . . what? Where is Ma Slessor going?"

At the word "twins," Ma Slessor had taken off into the forest like a startled deer with Okin hot on her heels. The rest of the villagers milled around, muttering angrily to one another.

Imatu was frightened. Among the Okoyong people, a twin birth meant the father of one of the babies must be an evil spirit, and that twin would grow up to be a monster if allowed to live. But since no one ever knew which twin was cursed, both were usually killed or put out in the forest to die, and the mother was driven out and shunned because of her great sin.

So what was the white Ma going to do? The whole village wanted to know. As darkness fell torches were lit, and everyone kept watch. One hour, then two went by. Then they heard the *thwack, thwack* of machetes cutting down vines and bushes. One of the village men trotted into the forest, then came back and reported: "It's Ma Slessor. She has the twin mother with her! But she is having Ma Eme's slave men cut a new path so the twin curse will not pollute our path to the village."

Imatu could tell the adults were upset and bewildered. Ma Slessor was bringing the twin mother to Ekenge? She was having a new path cut so that they didn't lose their own path into the forest? What did it mean?

Soon Ma Slessor came out of the forest, carrying a wooden gin case piled high with household cooking pots, followed by Ma Eme's slave woman, stumbling and frightened. Chief Edem cried out, "No, Ma Slessor! Don't come into our village with that twin woman!" But Ma Slessor marched right into the village with the box, into Chief Edem's compound, and into her hut.

The villagers crowded around—but not too close. Would their village be cursed if the twin mother stayed? What was Ma Slessor going to do?

A little while later, Ma Slessor came slowly out of her hut, carrying the box. But the cooking pots were gone. Instead, a small bundle wrapped in a cloth lay at the bottom of the box.

Ma Slessor looked around sadly. "Twins were born today at the farm of Ma Eme to a good woman, a good slave. She did nothing wrong. But she has been driven off the farm, all her belongings have been broken, and the babies were stuffed into this box along with her cooking pots. I brought her to my hut for safety. No one may touch her there."

The villagers were quiet, staring, wondering.

"One twin, a girl, still lives," Ma Slessor continued. "But the other twin, a boy, is dead . . . his head smashed by a cooking pot."

Imatu winced and looked over at Ma Eme. The chief's sister stood off to the side, a scowl on her wide face.

"I am going to give this baby a Christian burial. We can commit his soul to the tender mercies of the Heavenly Father, even in the wake of this great tragedy."

With that the Jesus teacher walked solemnly toward the forest edge. Several men stepped forward and broke up the ground with their machetes, then scraped aside the loose dirt. Chop, scrape, chop, scrape went the machetes. Finally a small hole was dug. Ma Slessor laid the bundle into the ground, and dirt was pushed back over the little body.

Immediately villagers began to wail and shout, but Ma Slessor yelled, "Stop!" Startled, everyone was quiet. Then, in a calm voice, Ma Slessor began to sing in Efik:

Be still my soul: the hour is hastening on
When we shall be forever with the Lord,
When disappointment, grief, and fear are gone,
Sorrow forgot, love's purest joys restored.
Be still my soul: when change and tears are
     past,
All safe and blessed we shall meet at last.

Stunned by the strange, quiet little funeral—so different from the drunken orgy at the village of Ifako last week!—the people walked quietly back to their compounds. But Imatu could hear angry murmurs about "the other twin" and "the twin mother."

"I don't know what everyone is upset about," Okin whispered in Imatu's ear as he came up alongside Imatu. "After all, Janie is a twin . . . and everyone seems to accept her."

Imatu stared at Okin, fear leaping up into her throat. Janie Slessor was a *twin*? Why had no one told her? She and Janie had played together, hugged each other, even eaten from the same dish.

If Janie was under a twin curse, had the curse come on Imatu, also?

Chapter 3

The Prank That Backfired

IMATU DIDN'T KNOW what to do. If she told her mother that Janie was a twin, Inyam might forbid her to play with the little girl. But Imatu was afraid of the twin curse; no one was supposed to associate with twins or the mother of twins. So when Janie called

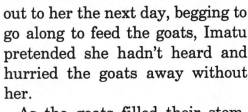

out to her the next day, begging to go along to feed the goats, Imatu pretended she hadn't heard and hurried the goats away without her.

As the goats filled their stomachs with the sweet grass from the small clearings in the forest, Imatu had time to think. So *that's* why Janie didn't know about her mother and father. Ma Slessor had probably rescued her from being killed at birth, just like she had rescued this new baby. Janie was already six years old and so pretty and sweet—she certainly didn't seem to have a twin curse on her. And Ma Slessor and the other children who related to Janie didn't seem to suffer any effects of the twin curse. . . .

Imatu had a sudden thought. The witch doctors said that only *one* twin is fathered by an evil spirit, but no one ever knows which one, so both are usually killed, just to be sure. But since Janie seemed no different than other children, the curse must have been on Janie's *twin*—not Janie herself.

That was it! Imatu was so relieved to figure it out that she rounded up the goats and headed back to the village earlier than usual. When she arrived, a crowd of men, women, and children were peering through the bamboo fence into the chief's compound. Okin saw Imatu return with the goats and ran over to her.

"Ma Eme and Ma Slessor are talking in the yard; they won't let anyone else in until they're done," he said excitedly.

But just then Ma Eme came out of the gate, her large bulk nearly filling the opening. Right behind her came Ma Slessor, her face beaming. Ma Eme stood with her hands on her hips and looked around at the curious faces.

"I have decided . . ." she said slowly, obviously not in a rush to satisfy the crowd's curiosity. "I have decided," she began again, "to take back my slave woman. She is a good woman and *if* . . ." Ma Eme let the word hang in the air for a moment. "If an evil spirit begat one of these twins, it wasn't the slave woman's fault." A noisy murmur went through the crowd, but Ma Eme glared at them, daring anyone to disagree with her. "But . . ."

The murmur stopped.

"But I will not take the twin baby that lives," sniffed Ma Eme. "Ma Slessor and I have made a compromise. I will take back the slave woman, and she will keep the baby. If the baby is cursed, the curse will be on her house and hers alone."

At this, the babble of voices rose to a high pitch. But Ma Slessor held up her hand, and again the crowd managed to quiet down.

The red-haired woman smiled happily. "I have named the baby Susie, in memory of my sister Susan—just as Janie is named in memory of my youngest sister. I am full of joy today that a precious life has been saved. And I promise you all that I will be a good mother to this child."

The crowd slowly drifted away, shaking their heads and muttering to one another. The white Ma certainly had some strange ways. Who ever thought that their village would allow a twin baby to stay alive—in the chief's compound at that!

The slave mother went back to Ma Eme's farm, taking some new household things, a gift from Ma

Eme. The newborn Susie—so tiny that she made baby Annie look huge!—thrived on cans of milk that Ma Slessor had among her many boxes. The rest of the villagers eyed the baby suspiciously but gradually accepted her presence, as long as Ma Slessor didn't ask anyone else to take care of her. So Janie and Okin now toted baby Annie about with them while Susie was rarely out of Ma Slessor's arms.

The little hut that Chief Edem had given her was much too crowded for a family of seven. "Chief Edem," Ma Slessor said to him one day. "I am deeply honored that you have given me a hut in your own compound. But would you give me a plot of land near the village where I can build a larger mission house? It would make your own compound less crowded," she said diplomatically.

The chief frowned thoughtfully and walked away. A few hours later he was back. "Ma Slessor, I have good news for you. I would like to give you a plot of land where you can build a larger mission house," he said, as if he had just thought of the idea. "I am honored that you have shared my compound, but you need more room for your growing family. This we would like to do to show our appreciation to you for coming and teaching us 'book.' "

When Okin told Imatu what the chief had said, he added slyly, ". . . *and* it gets the twin baby out of his compound." Imatu laughed. Okin had read her thoughts exactly!

True to his word, the chief gave Ma Slessor a plot of land—though he did not offer to help her clear it or build the house. Undaunted, Ma Slessor tied baby Susie on her back with a long strip of cloth, and for a few hours each day—when the rain stopped long enough—she and Okin whacked at the forest bushes, vines, and small trees with machetes to make a clearing.

The rest of each day, Ma Slessor went from compound to compound in the village, visiting with each of the women in turn, helping to pluck a chicken or weave a basket from tough grasses as they talked. The women were amazed and pleased that the Jesus teacher seemed genuinely interested in them and were soon chatting away about their babies, complaining about their husbands or children, or showing her new herbs to flavor the Okoyong diet of cornmeal and beans and hot peppers and fish.

All except Imatu's mother. Whenever Ma Slessor sat down by Inyam's hut to talk, the young widow became nervous and said little.

But one day, when Chief Edem, his son Etim, and some of the other village men were gone fishing, and Ma Eme had gone to visit her farm, Ma Slessor again came and sat down by Inyam's hut.

"Why are you afraid, my sister?" Ma Slessor said gently, touching the handsome woman gently on her arm.

Imatu was surprised to see her mother's eyes fill with tears. And then the whole story just seemed to spill out.

"My . . . my husband was the brother of Chief Edem's head wife," Inyam said, her voice quivering.

"We lived in the village of Akpo—about five miles from here—and I was the only wife to my husband, but my sister-in-law did not like me. When my . . . my husband drowned in a fishing accident, I was forced to take the *mbiam* oath to prove I had not put a curse on him and caused the accident. A chicken was slaughtered, and if it fluttered one way, I was innocent; if it fluttered the other way, I was guilty."

Imatu felt like putting her hands over her ears and running away. Her mother's words brought back the feelings of grief and terror following her father's death, like ripping open an old wound. But . . . it also felt good to have her mother tell Ma Slessor. Imatu wanted her to know! She wanted her to know about the sadness and fear and loneliness of living here in Ekenge. . . .

"I passed the test," Inyam went on. "So now by tradition my husband's relatives have to provide for me. This makes my sister-in-law angry. She has turned her husband, Chief Edem, against me. By Okoyong law, he has to give me protection in his compound, but he took all my inheritance as 'payment' for his hospitality."

Inyam's eyes narrowed and the tears stopped. "He treats me no better than one of his slaves, yet he expects me to be grateful. I hate him. *I hate him!*"

There. It was out. What would Ma Slessor say?

Ma Slessor sat beside Inyam silently for a long time. Then she said quietly, "It is not right. You have been treated unjustly."

Inyam looked startled. She had expected the

Jesus teacher to tell her she ought to be grateful to her benefactor.

"But, dear sister Inyam," Ma Slessor continued, "your hate only hurts you. You must forgive your brother-in-law. That is the way of Jesus."

Inyam shook her head and got up abruptly. "*Never*. I will never forgive him. He looks for ways to humiliate me. And one day . . . one day he will find a way to get rid of me—or kill me."

The beating of Etim's drum irritated Imatu. Several nights a week her cousin sat in the doorway of the boys' yard—where the older boys and unmarried young men lived when they got too old to live in the women's yards—and beat his drum. Usually the young men had been drinking gin, and they danced and laughed until late at night.

"Where do they get the gin?" Ma Slessor asked the chief crossly.

"Why, Ma, you know. The white traders sell us guns and slave chains and gin," the chief said, shrugging.

"What do you trade in return?" she demanded.

"Palm oil . . . a little rubber." The chief shrugged again. "We don't have much to trade."

"Nonsense!" Ma Slessor got all steamed up every time she and the chief had this conversation. "You have many rich resources in this delta between the Calabar and Cross rivers. And they have many good things you could trade them for besides gin!"

It was Ma Slessor's opinion that the young men drank because they were bored and didn't have enough to do. Okin grumbled to Imatu that Etim and the others just stood around and watched and drank while he and Ma cleared the little plot of land for the mission house.

But Imatu had her own reason for being upset when the young men drank: because they became insulting.

"Hey, chicken-legged girl!" they called out when Imatu went by with her goats. "You will have to stay in the fattening hut a whole year before anyone will marry *you*." Then they laughed, and her cousin Etim laughed hardest of all.

Imatu put her nose in the air and pretended not to hear them. But their insults hurt. She knew she was skinny, and that Okoyong men liked a fat wife best. What if no one wanted to marry her? Secretly, Imatu was glad she was skinny; she didn't want to get married anyway. But the boys' taunts also worried her. A single woman without a husband's protection was easy prey in the jungles of Okoyong.

"I wish I could take Etim's stupid drum and throw it in the river," Imatu complained to Okin one evening. Reading School was over, and the drumming and drinking and dancing in the boys' yard had begun. "He thinks he's better than anyone else."

Okin nodded in agreement . . . and then a slow grin lit up his face. "Why not?" he whispered. "We could sneak into the boys' yard when they fall asleep and take Etim's drum and hide it. No one would know what happened to it! That would teach him a lesson."

A thrill of excitement prickled the back of Imatu's neck. No girl was *ever* allowed in the boys' yard. But they all snored like sick cows after they'd been drinking. No one would ever know. And what a great trick to play on that stuck-up Etim!

It was hard to stay awake that night till the drumming and dancing stopped. But finally Imatu heard a quiet clicking sound outside her hut—Okin's signal. Hardly daring to breathe, she crawled out of her hut and followed Okin out of the chief's yard, across the village clearing in the darkness, to the gate of the boys' yard.

The gate was closed and Imatu suddenly got cold feet. They should go back to their own huts now, before they got caught! But Okin had already figured out how to unfasten the gate, and pulled it open before Imatu could run. He stepped inside the yard and motioned her to follow.

The moon was hidden by a thick blanket of clouds, and it was very dark inside the boys' yard. Imatu had never been inside the fence, but she thought she knew which was Etim's hut. Sure enough, Etim's spear that he had proudly decorated with colorful bird feathers was lying carelessly outside one of the huts. But no drum.

Okin motioned to Imatu to wait while he crept inside the hut and found the drum. Her heart was pounding so loudly in her ears she was sure it would

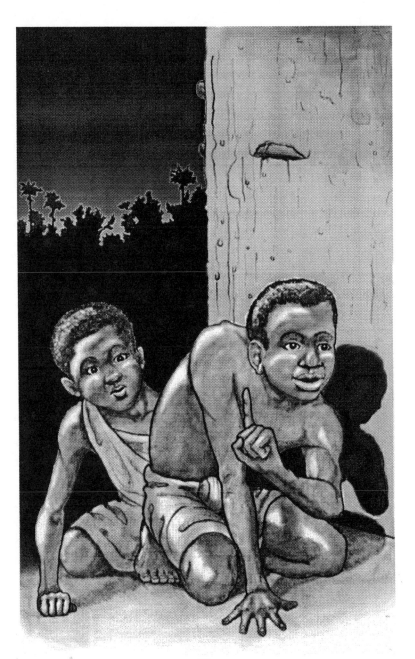

41

wake up the whole yard! *Why* had she and Okin planned such a stupid trick?

After what seemed like hours, Imatu saw a movement at the door of the hut. Okin was handing out the drum! Just as she took hold of it, however, she heard a big "Humpf!" from inside the hut . . . and then Etim's voice crying out loudly, "Wh—what? . . . Thief! Thief!"

Imatu turned and ran for the gate, the heavy drum thumping against her legs as she clutched the snakeskin strap. Was Okin behind her? She couldn't wait to find out! She had to get—

Whump! A dark figure jumped in her way and she crashed right into him.

She was caught!

Chapter 4

The Curse

E TIM KEPT SCREECHING, "Thief! Thief!" and soon the whole village was awake and stumbling into the clearing to see what was the matter. By the time Ma Slessor and Inyam arrived, torches had been lit, revealing the frightened faces of Okin and Imatu in the grip of Etim and one of the other young men who lived in the boys' yard.

"What is the meaning of this?" demanded Chief Edem, half-awake and bleary-eyed, wearing only a long sleeping shirt.

"These two—two *animals*," sputtered Etim, "came into my hut and stole my drum! See? The girl still has it in her hand!"

"Okin! Whatever put such a thing in your mind?" said Ma Slessor.

Okin hung his head. "We were only going to hide it—for a joke on Etim."

The other villagers, relieved that a real thief had not snuck into Ekenge, smiled and nodded. It was only a prank, a joke.

"Prank or not," scolded Ma Slessor, "you should never have done it." She turned to the chief. "I apologize for the behavior of my foster son, Chief Edem. I will see that he is punished."

Chief Edem seemed not to hear her but stood with his arms crossed, a scowl on his face. Finally he spoke. "A childish prank can be forgiven. But a more serious crime has been committed this night. The *girl*—this unruly, ungrateful girl that I have taken into my own compound—has violated a taboo: She has entered the boys' yard, which is expressly forbidden by Okoyong law!"

All the villagers turned and stared at Imatu. Suddenly she was very frightened; she wanted to run to her mother and hide her face in her skirt, like she used to do as a little girl when she was afraid. But the young man who had captured her still had her arm in a firm grip.

"Does everyone agree that the girl is guilty of entering the boys' yard?" asked the chief, looking around at the spectators.

There was a murmur of agreement.

"What is the penalty for violating this taboo?" asked the chief.

Imatu's whole body was shaking.

One of the older men stepped forward and cleared his throat. "The penalty for a female entering the boys' yard is one hundred lashes."

There was a stunned silence. Then Imatu's mother screamed. It took Ma Eme and another woman to hold her back as she writhed and sobbed.

"*One hundred lashes?*" cried Ma Slessor. "For a childish prank? The penalty is too severe! The child would die under that many lashes. *Two* lashes is enough—a lesson she will remember."

"Two? You make a joke! All the children will disobey the taboos if we don't punish the girl."

"Punish her, yes," argued Ma Slessor, hands on her hips, standing face-to-face with the chief. "But a punishment fit for a child."

Imatu was so terrified she could not utter a sound or even think. All she knew was that tonight she was going to die.

Back and forth the chief and Ma Slessor argued. The villagers looked at one another. Had anyone ever dared argue with the chief about a penalty for breaking a taboo? This was an amazing woman, this Ma Slessor!

Finally the chief snapped, "*Ten* lashes for breaking the taboo—and I will not give one less!"

Imatu's whole body shook with sobs as she lay on a mat in her mother's hut. Her back felt as if it were on fire from the ten lashes. She flinched when Ma Slessor gently put some cool ointment on the cuts and welts.

"Do you see now?" said Inyam in a voice thick with anger. "The chief hates us. One day he will kill us."

Ma Slessor did not answer right away but continued to treat Imatu's wounds. Then she said, "But a taboo *was* broken. The chief would have given a penalty to any girl who entered the boys' yard."

"Bah!" spat Inyam. "Taboos are broken, and sometimes they are punished, and sometimes the chief looks the other way."

"Yes, but when the whole village knows what has happened?" asked Ma Slessor gently. "Besides, he did finally agree to give only ten lashes instead of a hundred."

Inyam's temper flared. "You *agree* with lashing a young girl? Look at my daughter! She will have scars her whole life!"

"Agree? I certainly do not!" cried Ma Slessor. "It's an evil custom, and I will fight it with every ounce of my strength! But *ten* instead of a hundred is a giant step in the right direction. We must be grateful."

Inyam was silent as she squatted by the mat and stroked Imatu's head. Finally she spoke. "I *am* grateful to you, Ma, for standing up to the chief and demanding a lesser penalty. Only you could have done such a thing. He respects you. He respects this Jesus God you teach about. But I am *not* grateful to Chief Edem. That is exactly what he wants . . . to beat me down so low that I will be grateful when he 'only' beats my daughter ten times instead of a hundred!"

Imatu's wounds healed fairly quickly, and within a few days she was able to tend the goats as usual, but Okin would not be comforted. He could barely look Imatu in the eye. "It is all my fault, Imatu," he said gloomily on a visit to her hut with Ma Slessor and baby Susie. "I am the one who suggested we sneak into the boys' yard and take the drum."

Imatu struggled with her feelings. She resented the fact that both she and Okin had taken Etim's drum, but only she was given a whipping. Even worse than the terrible pain of the lash was the utter *humiliation*. Every time she saw her cousin Etim, he was mocking her. Right now Imatu didn't feel like having anything to do with boys at all—or anyone else for that matter—so she avoided Okin whenever possible. But she could see the sorrow in his eyes.

The rainy season finally ended in late October, and the warm, sunny months of the dry season were a welcome relief. Okin and Ma Slessor had almost finished clearing a place for the new mission house. The next step was to cut bamboo poles for the structure and find good mud to daub all over it.

But then Chief Edem developed an abscess—a festering sore on his back that made him very sick.

Immediately, Ma Slessor dropped everything else

47

to nurse the chief. She bathed his body with cool water to bring down the fever. She used some of her precious canned milk to get nourishment down his throat when he refused to eat. She boiled medicinal herbs, soaked rags in the brew, and applied poultices to the abscess, assisted by the large, comforting bulk of Ma Eme.

When her supply of herbs was all used up, she begged some from the other women in the chief's yard. But Inyam was reluctant to donate any of her own herbs. "Let him die," she muttered.

"Inyam!" Ma Slessor was shocked. "You must never say anything like that. Revenge is not the way of Jesus. Besides," Ma's voice became anxious, "someone might hear you."

"Well . . ." Inyam considered. "Imatu picks herbs for me when she goes with the goats. Maybe she could show you where to pick the ones you need."

So the next day, Ma Slessor left Ma Eme and the chief's head wife with instructions on how to put poultices on the chief's back, and went with Imatu and the goats to pick a fresh supply of herbs. All the Slessor children went, too, from Okin down to baby Susie.

At first Imatu felt awkward with Okin. She wanted to be his friend again, but she didn't know how to say it. When the goats stopped to eat, Udo and Okot and Janie ran on ahead, and Okin dropped behind with Imatu.

Okin spoke first. "Will you forgive me, Imatu, for getting you in trouble?" he said hopefully.

Forgive? Imatu wasn't sure what that meant. "It wasn't all your fault, Okin," she said slowly.

"But I *am* sorry, and it wasn't fair, and I want you to forgive me. That is the only way to make something right again—that's what Ma says. Just like Jesus forgives and washes us all clean inside when we are sorry for our sins."

Clean inside. How Imatu wished she felt clean inside! She was tired of all the anger and fear and loneliness.

"Yes, I—I forgive you . . ." she faltered, "and . . . and I want you to forgive me, too. For keeping you away."

A big grin spread over Okin's face. "I do! I forgive you!" And he laughed.

It was a wonderful day for Imatu. She had not realized how terribly lonely she'd been the past few weeks, not playing with or even speaking to the Slessor children. But now she pointed out the herbs Ma Slessor was looking for, milked one of the goats to give the children something to drink, and even carried baby Susie. She didn't even care that Susie was a twin.

When the happy little group trudged back into the village, however, they were met by an anxious Ma Eme.

"Careful, Ma Slessor," the big woman said under her breath. "Witch doctor has come." And then the chief's sister hurried away as quickly as she had come.

Ma Slessor gave baby Susie to Janie and hurried

toward the chief's hut. The witch doctor was sitting smugly outside the door, his face and body smeared with gray ashes. When the red-haired woman approached, he stood up and held out a bag.

"See what I have taken out of the chief's back?" he said accusingly, dumping the contents of the bag onto the ground. Ma Slessor and the children stared in amazement. There on the ground lay bird bones, animal teeth, pieces of eggshell, gun shot, various seeds, and a carved toothpick.

"Nonsense!" protested Ma Slessor. "Impossible."

"Very bad medicine," said the witch doctor, clucking his tongue. "Someone . . . someone has put a curse on him—"

"What?" protested Ma Slessor. "What are you talking about? Who called you to come? Who—?"

Just then the little group saw the chief's head wife slip away behind the hut.

"Never mind," sighed Ma Slessor. "But you must let me in to see the chief. I have fresh herbs to make poultices to draw the infection out of the abscess. Now step aside."

"You are mistaken!" scowled the witch doctor. "The chief will not get better until we discover who is to blame! Go away! You are not wanted here now." And he stood in the doorway, preventing Ma from entering. There was nothing Ma Slessor could do for the moment.

When time came for Reading School, only Imatu and Okin showed up. The rest of the village was milling around the witch doctor, wondering what he

was going to do.

It didn't take long to find out. Some of the men

built a fire in the middle of the village clearing. The witch doctor shuffled around it, chanting and mumbling to himself. Then he threw some powder into the flames; the fire sputtered and shot out sparks.

"Aiiieee!" cried the witch doctor. "The fire speaks. Someone is guilty of witchcraft . . . but who? Who makes an accusation?"

There was a hush. Then a voice cried out, "Inyam did it! The widow of my brother! She has no love for our chief!"

Imatu felt as if the breath had been knocked out of her. Why was the chief's head wife accusing her mother?

Two others were accused: a new slave woman and one of the chief's lesser wives. Immediately some of the warriors hurried into the chief's compound and dragged out the three women accused of witchcraft.

"Ma! Ma! What is happening!" screamed Imatu. "Stop them. They are putting chains on my mother."

Ma Slessor marched right past the witch doctor and the three prisoners and into the hut of Chief Edem.

"Chief! What is the meaning of this outrage?" she demanded. The chief was lying on his side, surrounded by smoking pots and feathers and necklaces of teeth—charms scattered around by the witch doctor.

"Go away, Ma Slessor," the chief moaned. "You mean well, but you do not understand these things. Have I ever had an abscess before? No! Someone has put a curse on me, and I will not get better until that person has been found out and punished."

"This is ridicu—"

"Get out, I say!" cried the chief, "or I will have you thrown out. Out! Out!"

Ma Slessor left, but she did not stay out. The next morning she was in the chief's hut, witch doctor or no witch doctor, pleading for him to release the prisoners. Twice more that day, she attempted to see the chief, to make him see the folly of chaining up prisoners instead of letting her treat his abscess with the fresh herbs.

The next time she came to the chief's hut, however, Ma Eme stood in the doorway. "You must stop pestering the chief, Ma Slessor," said the chief's sister, not unkindly. "He will see you no more."

"I will not stop!" cried Ma Slessor. "There are three innocent women chained to a pole in the middle of the village—and the chief's abscess is growing worse. Something is terribly wrong here!"

Ma Eme shrugged helplessly and did not move.

Imatu was afraid. She wanted to stay with her mother during the night, to make sure nothing happened to her, but the guards chased her away. So Ma Slessor took her into the crowded Slessor hut and let her sleep on a mat with little Janie.

Early the next morning, however, Imatu crept out to take some water to her mother. A few minutes later she was back, shaking Ma Slessor frantically. "Ma! Ma! Wake up!" she cried. "They are gone! My mother . . . the other prisoners . . . the guards . . . they have all disappeared!"

Chapter 5

Exiled

MA SLESSOR SCRAMBLED OUT OF HER HUT, followed by the older children. It was true; the village clearing was completely empty—no prisoners, no guards. The missionary hurried to the chief's hut to demand an explanation and made another startling discovery: The chief, his head wife, their son Etim, and the witch doctor were gone too! But where?

Running to Ma Eme's hut, Ma Slessor breathlessly told her friend about the missing persons. But the chief's sister just shrugged.

"My brother is stubborn," she said, calmly slicing a plantain into some sizzling palm oil over her breakfast fire. "He was tired of being pestered by you, so he took his family and the prisoners to his farm." The bananalike fruit turned crisp on the outside, mushy on the inside, and smelled delicious. Imatu's mouth watered, in spite of her anxiety about her mother.

But then the tone of Ma Eme's words changed. "He forbids you to follow him, Ma Slessor, or *all* the prisoners will be killed," she warned, shaking her finger.

Without a word, Ma Slessor turned and went back to her hut. *Is she going to give up so easily?* thought Imatu, scurrying along behind the slight, red-haired woman. She watched anxiously as Ma Slessor got the other children up, washed their hands and faces, put on fresh clothes, and fed them a breakfast of cold rice and dried fish. But just when Imatu had decided that Ma didn't care that her mother had disappeared, Ma Slessor took her and Okin aside.

"Okin," she said quietly, "I want you to go with Imatu and the goats today. Head in the direction of the chief's farm. When you find a good, grassy clearing, braid some vines and tie the goats so they can eat and lie down. Leave the goats while you find Chief Edem's farm and spy out what is happening. Then come and tell me. But be careful! Don't get caught."

Imatu was glad to have a plan—and glad for Okin's company. When they found a good spot for the goats to graze, they braided strong vines and tied the goats to some sturdy palm trees—not too close together, so they wouldn't get tangled up—just as Ma instructed. Then they headed in the direction of Chief Edem's farm.

Ma Eme had been speaking the truth. When the children finally located the chief's farm after a two-hour trek through the forest, Imatu could see her mother and the other two women prisoners, still in chains, harvesting cassava roots in one of the chief's garden plots. Okin crept closer to the huts but couldn't get close enough to hear anything.

That evening they reported what they'd seen to Ma Slessor.

"Hmm. If they are using the prisoners to work the farm, your mother does not seem to be in any immediate danger, Imatu," she said. "You must go each day, however, and bring me word. In the meantime, we must keep on with Reading School each evening, as if everything is normal."

For two more days, the children spied on the chief's farm and saw Inyam and the other prisoners working in the chief's garden. But on the fourth day, the prisoners were chained together near one of the huts. And this time they saw the witch doctor chanting and scattering charms all around another hut.

"What does it mean?" Imatu asked anxiously.

"I don't know," Okin said. "But we must go tell Ma—quickly."

As they had agreed, the children met Ma Slessor in the little cleared plot of land that the chief had given her for a mission house, so that no one would overhear them. When they described what they had seen that day, Ma Slessor paced back and forth. "The chief's abscess must be worse," she murmured, thinking out loud. "If he dies, they will kill all the prisoners and not bother to find out which one is supposedly 'guilty.' "

Imatu's heart seemed to crawl up into her throat.

The red-haired missionary kept pacing and thinking. Finally she stopped. "Okin, do you remember the Christian Calabar woman in Old Town who knows herb medicine?"

Okin nodded.

"This woman has treated many abscesses with much success," she explained to Imatu. "She may be our only chance. Okin, you must take a fishing canoe and go downriver to Old Town and persuade this woman to come with you. Say Ma Slessor asks her to come. Then take her straight to Chief Edem's farm. Do you think you can find it from the river?"

Again Okin nodded, his eyes shining with adventure.

"But do not take her all the way to Chief Edem's farm. The last mile she must go by herself, and just say she has heard that the chief is ill. Do you understand?"

That very evening, on the excuse that she was sending Okin to Old Town to purchase more canned milk for baby Susie, Ma Slessor packed some dried fish, fruit, and a cooked yam in a skin bag, gave him a few coins for the milk, and waved goodbye as the boy headed down the path toward the river.

Ma figured that, if all went well, Okin could arrive at Old Town by morning. He would need to rest, persuade the herb woman to come with him, and then paddle back upriver—which would take another day and night. Then the walk through the forest to the chief's farm . . . then back to Ekenge.

Two nights and two days . . . if all went well.

Sick with worry about her mother, Imatu found it hard to milk the goats, take them to the grassy places, boil rice and beans for her supper, and concentrate on the reading lesson during Reading School.

One day went by. On the second day, Imatu was tempted to tie up the goats and run through the forest to the chief's farm to see what was happening. But Ma Slessor had told her she absolutely must not do that. Her job was to wait.

Okin had not returned to Ekenge by the time she got back with the goats that afternoon. He was still not there when it was time for Reading School. But just as Imatu was getting ready to curl up on Janie's mat for the night, she heard whistling coming from the direction of the river path.

It was Okin! And he was carrying a box of canned milk on his head.

All had gone as planned. The Christian Calabar woman from Old Town had agreed to come with him, and he took her as close as he dared to Chief Edem's farm. Then he went back to the river to get the milk from the fishing canoe. And that was all. But one thing he knew: Imatu's mother and the other prisoners were still alive.

Now they had to wait.

Two more days went by. Then three. Still no word from Chief Edem. Imatu tossed and turned on her mat at night, worried about the fate of her mother. The only good thing was that Etim was also gone, and there was no annoying drumming coming from the boys' yard.

By the fourth day, Ma Slessor was as anxious as Imatu. "Okin, you must go with Imatu again today," she finally said, frowning. "Tie up the goats out in the forest once more and spy on the chief's farm."

Relieved to be able to *do* something besides wait, the two children did as Ma Slessor asked, and after tying the goats to graze, they crept close to the edge of the forest from where they could see the gardens and huts of the chief's farm in a sunny clearing. To their surprise, they were greeted by a flurry of activity. Bundles were being packed, fires put out . . . and the chief was standing up and walking around! Imatu looked around anxiously for a glimpse of her mother—and found her and the chief's lesser wife coming out of one of the huts carrying small bundles.

Okin poked Imatu. "Look!" he said, grinning. "No chains."

Imatu was weak with relief. But just then a movement on the far side of the clearing caught her eye. Out of the forest came two tall warriors. They did not look like Okoyong warriors, however. Where were they from? And what were they doing?

They watched one of Chief Edem's men go into a hut and bring out the third prisoner, the slave woman, still in chains. Chief Edem and the strange warriors met and talked, and then the tall warriors led the woman away.

Imatu's mouth went dry. "I think those were *Aros* warriors," she whispered to Okin.

"Aros? Who are they?" asked the boy.

Imatu swallowed hard. "From the north . . . they're cannibals. They eat people."

Ma Slessor went over again what Okin and Imatu had seen that day at Chief Edem's farm. "The chief looked healthy? And it looked like they were packing to come home?" The children nodded. "Praise to the Father of Light, who is stronger than the powers of darkness!" Ma exclaimed. "But . . . you say the slave woman was taken away by Aros warriors?"

More nods.

"I wonder what that rascal chief is up to," Ma Slessor muttered.

Chief Edem and his party walked into the village just as Reading School was finishing that evening. The chief smiled broadly at Ma Slessor. "See, Ma?" he said cheerfully. "I am better now. The old ways are best, you see?" And without waiting for a reply, he retired to his hut.

With a grateful cry, Imatu ran to her mother and gave her a big hug. "Oh, Mem, Mem, you have returned safely!" she cried.

But Inyam did not smile. She loosened Imatu's grip and pushed her back so that she could look at

61

her. "We are being sent away," she said dully.

"*What?*" cried Ma Slessor, who had also come over to greet Inyam. "Sent away? But why?"

Inyam just picked up a bundle with one hand, took Imatu's hand with the other, and walked toward their hut. Bewildered, Imatu looked back over her shoulder at Ma Slessor, Okin, and the other children. What was happening?

That night Imatu lay on her mat, listening to Etim's drum coming from the boys' yard. She had thought that when her mother returned home safely, everything would be all right again! But something was wrong. What did her mother mean, "sent away"?

Maybe Imatu had misunderstood. Maybe she meant that the slave woman had been sent away. That must be it.

But the next morning Inyam told Imatu to begin rolling their sleeping mats as she packed their cooking pots, baskets, and clothes. Ma Slessor, with baby Susie on her hip, watched the pile of bundles growing outside Inyam's hut, then marched over to the chief's hut.

"Chief Edem!" she called. "I have missed you. Now that you are well, let's sit and have a *palaver*— so much has happened while you were away; there are so many things to talk about."

Looking relieved that Ma Slessor did not seem to be angry with him, the chief came out of his hut and sat down on one of Ma Slessor's stools that she brought out of her hut. Several other villagers gathered around to hear the chief and Ma talk. Imatu slipped away from her mother's packing and crept close to the *palaver*.

Ma expressed her happiness that the chief was feeling better and had returned to the village. She then described her plans for the mission house she was building—the dimensions had been marked on the ground, and the next step was to gather bamboo for the frame and mud for the walls. The chief nodded his approval.

Ma offered to tutor the chief personally so that he could catch up with the rest of the Reading School now that he was well. Again the chief seemed pleased.

"But, Chief Edem," the missionary said abruptly, "you went away with three prisoners and only two have come back. What happened to the other slave woman?"

The chief squinted into the morning sunlight, as if he hadn't heard her question. After a few minutes, however, he said, "Oh, she ran away. But she was a worthless slave anyway, so I let her go."

Imatu shot a sharp look at Okin. Ran away? They knew better! Then she realized that Ma Slessor could say nothing about the slave woman being given to the cannibal warriors or the chief would know someone had been a spy—and suspected spies would be subjected to the poison bean ordeal!

Ma Slessor changed the subject. "Why are you sending away the woman Inyam and her daughter Imatu?"

The chief squirmed a little—then lifted his chin defiantly. "Because I am chief and must do what is best for the whole village! The kinswoman of my wife does not appreciate what I have done for her, taking her into my own compound and giving her protection. Already there have been two incidents threatening the well-being of my family—"

"*Two* incidents?" Ma Slessor interrupted. "If you mean taking Etim's drum, that was an innocent joke! And the girl has already been punished enough. As for the abscess you suffered, it was a natural infection that has now healed. You *know* that Inyam did not cast any witchcraft spell on you!"

Chief Edem stood up in frustration. "Ma, you mean well, but you do not understand these things. Sickness and accidents—these things are not natural! A wise chief must get rid of evil influences. The woman and the girl must go—today!" With that, the chief stalked away.

Ma Eme, who had been standing nearby, stopped Ma Slessor from running after the chief. "My brother has spoken," she warned. "At least Inyam is leaving with her life. You have influenced him more than you know."

Ma Slessor sighed and caught Imatu's eye. The girl's face registered her shock and dismay.

"Ma! What does he mean? Where will we go? What about Reading School?" Tears welled up in Imatu's eyes.

Ma Slessor shook her head and walked over to Inyam, who continued to stack her belongings outside of the hut. "Where will you go, Inyam?" she said gently to the handsome woman. "What will you do?"

Inyam straightened, her face betraying no emotion. "We will go back to Akpo, our old village. My sister's husband may be willing to give me some land to farm. Imatu and I know how to work hard. We will survive. Maybe it is best. I do not want to live where I am not wanted."

Okin handed Imatu the braided vine tied around the neck of the goat. "I will miss you, Imatu," he said awkwardly.

Imatu dug her toes into the dirt. A big lump tightened her throat, and tears threatened to spill down her cheeks. She didn't want to say goodbye. Ma Slessor and Okin and little Janie were the only friends she had.

No one else from the village had come to the edge of the forest to say goodbye to Inyam and Imatu. Only Etim leaned against a tree in the distance, a mocking smile on his face, idly thumping his drum. Imatu looked at Ma Slessor holding little Annie on one hip and baby Susie on the other. Three-year-old Okot and eight-year-old Udo were clinging to her skirts. But . . . where was Janie?

"Goodbye, Inyam," said Ma Slessor softly. "Goodbye, Imatu. The God of love will go with you."

Inyam just said, "Come on, Imatu. We must leave."

Imatu tugged on the vine and started down the path after her mother with the goat in tow.

"Imatu! Imatu! Wait . . . wait!" cried a familiar voice. Janie came flying around the edge of the village. Her arms were full of flowers—orchids and jasmine and orange blossoms.

Panting, the little girl tucked the lush bouquet in a fold of Imatu's skirt. "For you," she said shyly. "I love you."

The tears finally spilled over. No one had ever said "I love you" to Imatu before. And the sweet words had come from Janie—a twin supposedly under a "curse."

Chapter 6

Baskets and More Baskets

IMATU STRAIGHTENED UP and stretched her aching back. The tropical sun shone hot and unrelenting in the little clearing where she and her mother were planting rows of beans. Mopping her face with her head scarf, Imatu thought longingly of the shady forest where she used to take Chief Edem's goats when they lived in Ekenge. But now . . . .

It had been four months since she and her mother had been exiled from Chief Edem's village. Their old village of Akpo had been reluctant to take them back. Two more women's mouths to feed! But Inyam had been determined to pay her own

way. She rented a patch of land from her sister's husband, promising to pay him with part of the first crop. Then she begged small amounts of seeds from several families until she had enough to plant a few rows of beans, corn, yams, cassava root, and even some rice in a swampy patch near a creek—enough to feed her and Imatu. In the meantime, Inyam hired herself out to various village farms in exchange for food until she could harvest her own meager crops.

"Hurry up, Imatu!" called Inyam impatiently, loosening the ground ahead of Imatu with her machete. "There will be time to rest when the seeds are in."

Imatu sighed and retied her head scarf. It was April—time for the wet season to begin, and they had to get the seeds planted before the rains came. She poked several beans in the ground and made a little mound where the bush would grow, then she took a few steps and poked several more beans in the ground.

"Hello-o-o! Hello!" called a voice. "Inyam! Imatu!"

Imatu jerked her head up. That sounded like Okin! She jumped up and scanned the edge of the forest. Sure enough, there was Okin running down the path carrying a bundle, and behind him she could see Ma Slessor—barefoot and hatless, as usual—with baby Susie tied on her back.

A big grin spread on Imatu's face. Ma Slessor had not forgotten them. At least cnce a month she and some of her children had walked through the forest the five miles from Ekenge to Akpo to see them. Old

Chief Akpo—after whom the village was named—had heard that Ma Slessor was a wise woman and a fair judge. He welcomed her visits and invited her to judge family disputes or cases when Okoyong law was broken. And at each visit, Okin had tried to teach Imatu what they'd been learning in Reading School—but Imatu felt frustrated and sad that she couldn't be learning every day.

Today Ma Slessor immediately began helping Inyam break up the ground with her own machete. "I'll help you plant the beans," Okin said to Imatu. Imatu knew her mother would be pleased, even if she didn't say so. That was Ma Slessor's way: When she visited any family, she always pitched right in and helped with the work, so that her visit was a help instead of a hindrance.

With four people working, the rows of beans were soon planted, and the little work party collapsed in the shade at the edge of the forest. Inyam laid out some flat bread and beans seasoned with red peppers that she had brought for their noon meal; Ma Slessor and Okin contributed two juicy mangoes and some dried fish.

"It's a picnic!" laughed Ma Slessor, bouncing baby Susie on her lap. "Just like we used to have back home in Scotland."

"Speaking of Scotland," said Okin slyly, "I have a treat for you, Imatu—it came in the missionary box from Ma's home church."

He unwrapped some hard, round, pink things and put them in Imatu's hand. "Suck it," he urged.

Imatu put one of the hard things in her mouth. Oh! It was so sweet and good!

Okin grinned. "It's peppermint candy! The children in Scotland sent them for Ma Slessor's children—*and* our friends."

"And I have a present for you, Inyam," said Ma Slessor, pulling a smaller bundle out of Okin's bag. "It's cotton cloth—to make clothes for you and Imatu."

Inyam's eyes grew big. She gently touched the soft, green cloth. It had pretty pink and gold flowers scattered all over it. She held it close to her body, where it made a sharp contrast with the drab, brown, tattered garment she was wearing.

"That came in the missionary box, too," Okin said.

"But that is not the real reason I came," Ma Slessor said, her tone becoming very businesslike. "I want to talk to you, Inyam, about trading Okoyong goods with the people of Calabar along the seacoast."

Inyam gave Ma Slessor a puzzled look. "Trade? You mean like the white traders who come up the Calabar River and trade guns and gin and slave chains for some of our palm oil and rubber?"

Ma Slessor put her hands over her ears and gave a little screech. "That is exactly what I want to change!" she cried. "Bullets and alcohol and chains only make your lives more miserable! But there are many things the Okoyong people could trade for that would give you a better quality of life—cloth and tools and household goods and cooking utensils and medicine and even doors and windows for your huts!

And there are wonderful resources here in the rain forest that you could use for trade: rubber and palm oil and peanut oil and woven baskets—"

"Baskets!" snorted Inyam. "Every woman weaves her own baskets to hold the yams she digs or to carry clothes down to the creek to wash. No one would trade beautiful cloth like this"—she held up the soft material Ma Slessor had given her—"for my plain old baskets."

"But you're wrong, Inyam," said Ma Slessor. "Your baskets are beautiful and well made. The women in the towns downriver don't have time to make their own baskets. They have to help their husbands in the marketplace or clean the fish their husbands catch at sea. They would rather trade or pay money for good-quality baskets to use at home or in their shops."

Inyam stared at her.

Ma Slessor got up, brushing dirt and grass from her skirt. "Will you think about it, Inyam? I must also go talk to your chief. If the young men from Ekenge and Ifako and Akpo work hard to get the sap from lots and lots of rubber trees, they can trade for many things that would help their villages—*and* they won't have so much time to drink gin and get into fights with each other!"

The stack of baskets inside the hut was growing. Each day after hoeing their little farm plot and milking the goat, Imatu would go hunting for sturdy, long reeds and grasses, which Inyam wove into baskets of different shapes. Then her mother would soak the finished baskets in water and let them dry until they were tight as a drum.

Some of the other women in Akpo thought Inyam was crazy. "Why do you make so many baskets? You will not be able to give them away!" they laughed.

Inyam ignored their comments. "My daughter and I are working like slaves, even though I am a free woman," she retorted. "If Ma Slessor is right, I will be able to trade for things we need and won't have to work night and day just to put a little food into my daughter's belly."

One day when Imatu was out in the forest hunting for reeds, she popped some juicy berries into her mouth . . . then stared thoughtfully at the red stain they left on her fingers.

"Mem! Look at this!" she cried when she got back to their hut. She unfolded a large leaf and poured out a handful of berries into a clay bowl. She pounded the berries with a stone, making a thick, red liquid. Then, dipping a green twig into the red liquid, Imatu carefully smeared the red color along one of the woven rows on a basket.

Her mother watched, fascinated. "Do another," she urged.

Imatu painted another ring around the basket. Inyam was pleased—and so was Ma Slessor the next time she came to visit and saw all the different designs and colors Imatu had painted on various baskets. "This is wonderful!" she exclaimed. "You must both come with me when we go downriver to trade in Creek Town. Yes—it's about time to set up our first trading expedition and go to meet King Eyo!"

The constant summer rains had made the path through the forest from Akpo to Ekenge slippery with mud. Monkeys screeched in the treetops as Inyam and Imatu carefully picked their way through the dripping bushes, ferns, and rotting leaves on the forest floor. Both the woman and the girl carried a large bundle of baskets tied together with vines.

Imatu was excited. Tomorrow they were going by canoe downriver to Creek Town—and would meet King Eyo Honesty himself! And in just a few hours she would get to see little Janie Slessor—as well as Okin and the other Slessor children.

But as they got closer to Ekenge, Imatu's excitement changed to worry. "Mem . . . Mem!" she called, trying to keep her balance as she stumbled on a large tree root. "What if Chief Edem is angry that we are returning to his village? What will he do to us?"

"You heard Ma Slessor," Inyam reminded her. "She told us to come straight to her new mission house on the edge of the village. The mission house is a refuge—no one will dare hurt us there."

Even though Okin had told Imatu that Ma Slessor had finally built a two-room mission house on the piece of land Chief Edem had given her, Imatu was still surprised to see the large, rectangular hut sitting on the little clearing. Janie and Udo and Okot came squealing down the path to meet them. Ma Slessor stood smiling in the doorway, baby Susie on her hip as usual.

"Guess what?" Okin whispered to her as they put down their big bundles of baskets. "Etim is getting married. He's actually clearing land to build himself and his new wife a hut!"

Imatu just made a face. She didn't care what her cousin Etim did—although it would be a sight to see him actually *working*.

"Such a fine house," Inyam murmured as she walked slowly through the two-room mud house, stepping over an old, sick woman lying on a mat in the sleeping room and gently touching Ma Slessor's sewing machine, which the missionary used to sew simple garments for the village women and children.

"And look!" Janie pointed proudly. "A dish cupboard and something to sit on!"

Imatu was amazed. One mud wall had been scooped out to make several flat shelves for Ma Slessor's dishes and cooking pots. A fireplace in one corner had a mud chimney so the smoke could go outside. But most amazing of all was a mud "bench" built right against a wall, with a soft pad on the seat that Ma Slessor had sewn. A runaway slave woman nursing her year-old baby was occupying this wonderful piece of furniture.

Ma Slessor nodded. "We are very grateful to have

this house . . . but as you can see, it is already too small. I am thinking of building on more rooms—or even making it two stories high! Many come who are sick or need refuge."

Imatu was only half listening. On the wall hung a photograph of a handsome white man, a pretty white woman, and two children. "Who is it, Ma?" she asked.

Ma Slessor started to answer, but Okin jumped in. "That man was a mean bully when he was my age. He tried to scare Ma to keep her from teaching the Bible to orphans on the street in Scotland—"

"And he swung a heavy stone on a cord closer and closer to her head, but she didn't run away!" Udo interrupted.

"Is that true, Ma?" Imatu asked.

Ma Slessor smiled and nodded. "I made that bully a deal. If he couldn't scare me, then he had to listen to my Bible lesson! When the stone scraped my forehead, he was so ashamed that he made his whole gang come to my Bible class. Now he's all grown up, and he sent me that picture of his family to thank me for introducing him to Jesus. I keep it there to remind me how Jesus can change a young person's life—even someone as young as you, Imatu."

Ma Slessor gave Imatu a warm hug, then bustled around organizing supper for her huge household—twelve adults and children tonight! "We must get to sleep early—we have a long journey tomorrow," she said. "Several chiefs and men from all three villages will be going along bringing goods to trade."

Imatu shivered even though the damp evening was warm. She was both scared and excited. Whoever thought she would see Creek Town and meet the king who had loaned Ma his royal canoe!

Chapter 7

The Accident

EARLY THE NEXT MORNING, the whole village of Ekenge gathered at the riverbank in the rain to send off the people going to Creek Town. The chiefs of Ifako and Akpo were also there, along with several men from each village taking things to trade.

Okin was being left behind to take care of Udo, Janie, Okot, and the mission house guests—under the watchful eye of Ma Eme. There was some muttering about why the woman Inyam was going, but Ma Slessor made it clear that Inyam had no husband to support her, so she must represent herself. As for Imatu, Ma Slessor needed help with the babies—Annie and Susie—and that settled that.

77

Everyone was yelling advice.

"Put all the goods in one canoe and tow it behind the other."

"Idiot! Each canoe needs its own paddlers. Chiefs in one, women in the other—and divide the paddlers."

"Don't stack those baskets that way! Any child can see you have to do it like this."

"Bring back cloth for dresses!"

"No! We need more weapons."

In spite of all the advice, both canoes were finally loaded to the rim with a barrel of palm oil, large balls of raw rubber, baskets of yams and plantains, a bag of palm kernels, some gifts for King Eyo, and Inyam's baskets. But as the men stepped forward to get into the canoes, Ma Slessor shouted, "Stop!"

She looked the men up and down. Each one was wearing a sword or carrying a spear or gun. "*No weapons,*" she said firmly. "We are going as peaceful traders—not warriors. Leave them behind."

There was an immediate uproar. "What? No Okoyong man goes to a strange place without his weapon!"

But Ma Slessor sat down on the riverbank and said stubbornly, "We don't leave until the weapons stay."

For an hour the men argued. "You want to make women of us, Ma!" they complained. Mary Slessor just sat. Another hour went by. Some of the men stalked off angrily, including Chief Akpo, to the cheers of the crowd.

But finally Chief Edem, the chief from Ifako, and the remaining men reluctantly laid down their weapons and got in the canoes. One of the canoes was so overloaded that it immediately tipped over, causing another uproar until all the trade goods had been fished out of the river, the canoe drained, and everything repacked.

As Ma Slessor got into one of the canoes, she noticed several spears sticking out of a long bundle hidden on the bottom. Grabbing the spears, she pitched them out onto the riverbank. "I said no weapons! And I mean no weapons!"

Finally, to the wails and shouts of those being left behind, the two canoes were pushed away from the bank. Imatu sat in the middle of one with baby Annie. Her mother and Ma Slessor sat in the middle of the other, taking turns caring for baby Susie and using a paddle.

They were off.

The trip down the Calabar River to Creek Town took twelve hours, and it was dark before they pulled the canoes up onto the narrow beach. A runner had alerted King Eyo that Ma Slessor and the Okoyong visitors were coming, so they were met at the beach by men with torches to light the way to the king's house.

The king's house was not made of mud but of wood and stone, with tiles on the roof instead of palm branches. Imatu had never imagined such shiny floors—and real furniture to sit on! They were all given fresh fruit and chicken and plenty of rice to eat and a blanket to sleep on for the night. But Imatu was too excited to sleep much.

The next day they met with the king. Imatu hadn't expected the king to be a dark Calabar man dressed in European clothes and a top hat. He was accompanied by several Calabar chiefs, dressed in traditional, full robes and brightly colored hats.

King Eyo and Ma Slessor exchanged warm words and handshakes, then Ma politely introduced each individual who had come along on the trading expedition. Chief Edem was so delighted to meet the king that he jabbered away nonstop for ten minutes about the king's fine house and his unusual clothes and how the king *must* come to Ekenge in his royal canoe for a visit. Then, to impress the king, he bragged about how many wives and slaves he had, how many hunts he'd been on, and how he was the most important chief in Okoyong because Ma Slessor had chosen to live in his village.

Imatu noticed that the fancy Calabar chiefs were whispering and chuckling at Chief Edem's foolish talk. The king noticed also and scolded them gently. "The Gospel, which has made you what you are, has only recently been taken to Okoyong by our dear Ma. These are our guests, and we must honor them for the sake of our Lord and Savior."

King Eyo then graciously invited the Okoyong visitors to come to the Calabar Christian church in

Creek Town that evening, where he himself preached. Afterward, Imatu overheard the Ifako chief telling Chief Edem: "Ma Slessor has been wanting to build a church school in Okoyong. I will donate land near Ifako, and it will be a church for both our villages. What do you say, eh?"

Two days later, as the Okoyong canoes headed upriver, Imatu's head was full of all the sights and sounds of the trading expedition to Creek Town. The marketplace had been wonderful! Besides local fruits, vegetables, and live animals to trade, there had also been goods from other countries—cloth and shoes and chairs and tea and spices and tools and glass windows. Her mother's baskets sold quickly, and many people grunted approvingly when they saw the designs that Imatu had painted on them. Many people paid in coins. At first Inyam didn't know what to do with them and was afraid she was being cheated. But then Ma Slessor showed her how she could take the coins and buy things she wanted in the market.

Imatu nudged the bamboo cage at her feet that held the four hens and one rooster her mother had purchased. Now they would have eggs to eat along with their beans and rice and yams! Her mother had also bought or traded for some more cloth, seeds to plant, and a large metal pot.

Imatu sighed contentedly, careful not to disturb little Annie who lay on her lap, lulled to sleep by the swish, swish of the canoe paddles. She had so much to tell Okin and Janie! Of course, they had seen it all before, but now she could share it with them.

The trip upriver took longer than the trip down, and it was the middle of the night before the two canoes nosed up on the little landing beach in Okoyong. It wasn't easy unloading the canoes in the dark, but the job was almost finished when Ma Slessor spoke. "What is that? I hear something."

Everyone stopped and listened. Then they saw it—a light bobbing toward them down the path from Ekenge. And then they heard a voice calling: "Ma! Ma Slessor! Oh, Ma, come quickly!"

Within moments, a small figure carrying a torch ran out of the forest and down the riverbank.

"Okin!" cried Ma Slessor. "What is it? What is the matter?"

Okin's eyes were wide with fright. "There's been an accident! It's .. it's Etim! A log fell on him and he can't move!"

Ma Slessor sank onto the mud "bench" in the mission house and wearily closed her eyes. She had been up the rest of the night with Etim and had only come back to the house to get some fever medicine from her supplies.

"Here, my friend, you must eat something," said Inyam, handing Ma Slessor a cup of goat's milk and some corn mush that she had prepared for all the children. While Chief Edem and Ma had kept the long night vigil with the paralyzed Etim, Inyam and

Imatu had put the babies to sleep in the mission house and comforted the other children, who were frightened by all the confusion.

"Etim is supposed to marry a girl from Ifako next month, you know," Okin had tried to explain. "He was chopping down a tree to build his new hut when something happened . . . the log slipped and hit Etim on the back of the neck. When the men pulled it off, Etim couldn't move. They carried him back to the village . . . and . . . and I was sent to tell the chief and Ma as soon as the canoes got back."

Imatu was upset by the news. She didn't like Etim very much, but she had never wanted anything so terrible to happen to him. But other feelings competed with concern for her cousin. She felt resentful that her excitement about the trip to Creek Town and meeting King Eyo and trading their baskets for many new things seemed unimportant now. And underneath all the other feelings was a vague, unsettling fear. . . .

"Thank you, Inyam," sighed Ma Slessor, handing back the empty bowl and cup. "I'm sorry our trip has ended this way. But . . . I think you should go back to your own village right away. Etim is very bad, and if he dies there's going to be trouble. The chief believes no violent death happens except by witchcraft. I don't know what will happen—but I think it'd be best if you weren't here."

Inyam seemed relieved to have permission to leave and quickly began packing her things.

"But," Ma continued, "I have a favor to ask. Could

Imatu stay with me for a few days? I must stay close to Etim . . . and Imatu could be a big help with the babies. That is," she turned to Imatu, her eyes pleading, "if you would be willing, Imatu."

Imatu looked uneasily at her mother. She felt pleased that Ma Slessor wanted her help . . . and taking care of Annie and Susie was a lot more fun than chopping weeds on their farm plot. But she felt afraid—afraid to stay in Ekenge near an angry Chief Edem, afraid to be away from her mother.

Inyam was silent for several moments. Then she nodded. "You have done much for us, Ma Slessor. We will do this for you." She picked up the cage of chickens in one hand, slung the bundle of her other goods from Creek Town over her back, and with a brief wave, disappeared quickly into the forest.

Imatu knew there was going to be trouble when the witch doctor arrived.

Two weeks had passed, and Etim hung between life and death. Most of the time he was unconscious or delirious. The red-haired missionary stayed by the injured boy's side almost constantly day and night. Daily she tried to feed him a nutritious broth, but most of it ran out of Etim's mouth.

And then the witch doctor arrived. That night the drums began beating. The villagers built a huge fire in the village clearing and began to drink a great deal of gin.

Exhausted, Ma Slessor was persuaded by Ma Eme to get a few hours sleep. But listening to the drums, Ma was anxious. "Keep watch," she urged Okin and Imatu. "Wake me if anything happens."

Imatu and Okin crept to the edge of the village clearing, where they could watch the fire without being seen. The witch doctor danced slowly around the fire while the worried chief and many of the villagers watched and drank. The chanting and dancing went on for hours, it seemed. And then suddenly the witch doctor shouted some words that Imatu didn't understand.

A few minutes later, four men appeared carrying something between them. Imatu almost cried out. It was Etim! The men laid the young man down on the ground near the fire. The witch doctor and several of the older men began shouting in Etim's ear, trying to wake up his spirit. They sucked on pipes and blew smoke up his nose. Then they dipped their fingers into a bowl and rubbed something into his eyes.

"Get Ma—quick!" Imatu whispered fiercely into Okin's ear. With her heart beating wildly, she continued to watch from the shadows. Suddenly Etim's body began to convulse violently. And then—just as suddenly—the convulsions stopped.

The drumming and the dancing and the shouting stopped. There was dead silence.

Then a bloodcurdling scream pierced the night air. "He is dead!" shrieked Chief Edem. "My son is dead! Sorcerers have killed him, and they must die!"

At his words, all the village men and women who

had been watching disappeared. No one's life was safe when a witch-hunt was declared. In the middle of the clearing, Etim's mother—the chief's head wife—threw her body on top of her son, wailing with grief.

A cool hand touched Imatu's shoulder, and the girl nearly screamed with fright. She looked up into the worried face of Ma Slessor, who put a finger to her lips.

Meanwhile the witch doctor was shaking a leather bag. With a flourish he shook out several small stones and studied the way they fell on the ground. He raised his arms high, casting a long, dancing shadow in the firelight. "The stones do not lie!" cried the witch doctor. "Someone in a nearby village has cursed the chief's family, and now his son is dead."

Hearing his declaration, a few of the villagers crept back into the circle. One of the men said, "Chief Akpo was angry when Ma Slessor told us to leave our weapons behind when we went to Creek Town. He left and did not return."

Heads nodded and voices murmured angrily. Then someone else spoke up. "Akpo! That is where the chief's sister-in-law lives since he sent her away!"

Imatu began to tremble. She heard voices shouting her mother's name. "Inyam! Yes! Yes! Inyam returned to trade with us at Creek Town . . . and then the accident happened!"

"Akpo! That is the village responsible for our trouble!"

Imatu felt Ma Slessor's arms go around her, and

then she breathed urgently into Imatu's ear, "You must run, Imatu—run to Akpo and warn your mother. Warn the whole village!"

Imatu's heart seemed to leap into her throat. "But it is night! The dark . . . the wild animals . . . it is five miles—"

"Go *now*! Your mother's life depends on it!"

Stifling a frightened cry, Imatu ran toward the yawning mouth of the forest.

Chapter 8

The Regal Corpse

DRIVEN BY TERROR, Imatu's feet flew over the path toward Akpo. She could hardly see where she was going, but she stumbled blindly along, pushing aside vines and bushes that seemed to slap her face and tear at her clothes.

After the first headlong rush into the forest, Imatu knew she couldn't run all five miles. She slowed to a walk, trot . . . walk, trot. *Don't think about Chief Edem's threat,* she told herself. *Don't think about the dark forest. Just keep walking fast.*

Somewhere in the forest a panther screamed. Raw fear threatened to freeze Imatu in her tracks, but

she forced herself to go on. She mustn't think about wild animals . . . she mustn't think . . . she mustn't think. . . .

Imatu jumped at a strange, small sound—almost like a baby's weak cry. Maybe it was the panther's cub, whimpering for its mother. If so, she must keep going . . . walk, trot . . . walk, trot . . . mile after mile. . . .

Just when she thought she must have taken a wrong turn, the path spilled out of the forest into a large clearing. A damp smoke from a dozen smoldering fires hung over the sleeping village of Akpo. And there was her mother's hut, sitting by itself on the edge of the village, and the goat, penned in its little yard.

"Wake up! Wake up!" shouted Imatu, running through the village. "Warriors are coming! You must run . . . run! Into the forest! Wake up! Run, run!"

Villagers stumbled out of their huts. "What warriors?" they demanded. "What has happened?"

"Chief Edem's son . . . is dead," Imatu gasped. "They think Akpo . . . is guilty of putting a curse on him!"

"Look! Look!" someone yelled. "They're coming now!" All eyes turned toward the forest, where the darkness now glittered with the bobbing light of approaching torches.

There was immediate confusion. Fathers and mothers grabbed sleeping children and ran into the forest. Goats bleated and chickens squawked. People were running . . . stumbling . . . grabbing weapons and clothes and food—whatever they could carry.

Imatu ran to her mother's hut. It was empty.

The young girl panicked. Where was her mother? But she couldn't wait to hunt for her—the bobbing torches were almost to the village. Maybe her mother already got away. Without looking back, Imatu ran into the forest.

Behind her she heard the Ekenge warriors give a shrill war cry, followed by the shouts and shrieks and cries of the villagers.

A few minutes later, a brilliance lit up the forest. Imatu stopped running, circled back cautiously, and peered through the leafy bushes into the clearing.

Akpo was burning.

The Ekenge warriors were setting all the huts on fire. She could see people still running and screaming, being chased by warriors. Some were caught and herded together in a group away from the village.

Imatu's heart beat loudly in her ears. Where was her mother? Did she get away?

On the edge of the village, Imatu could see her mother's hut—the hut Inyam had worked so hard to build—burning brightly along with the others.

Imatu slumped to the ground, hidden by the bushes and the night. She suddenly felt very alone and scared.

Imatu woke with a start. Her body felt stiff and cramped. Daylight had come, but the only noise was the squawking parrots and chattering sunbirds in the treetops overhead.

The village of Akpo lay silent . . . or what used to be the village. All that remained were charred bamboo fences and smoldering lumps of palm branches that had caved into the mud huts.

Then Imatu heard another noise . . . a familiar bleat. Blinking her eyes against the sunlight, she watched as a goat wandered out of the forest, looking confused and unhappy. It stumbled around the edge of the smoking village, bleating now and then as if to say, "Is anybody here?"

Imatu waited. Five minutes . . . ten minutes. But she saw no one else. Cautiously, she crept out from under the bush and stepped into the clearing.

Was it her mother's goat? Imatu wasn't sure. But because she didn't know what else to do, she braided a vine, tied it around the goat's neck, and started back down the path . . . back to Ekenge.

Imatu led the goat the five miles to Ekenge in a kind of daze. Her mad run through the night . . . had it done any good? Had she warned the people in time? Some people had been caught . . . but what about her mother? Had she gotten away? The need to know kept Imatu's feet plodding ahead, one after the other, even though she was afraid of what she might find when she got back to Ekenge.

Even before she reached the village, Imatu could hear the death drums and a great commotion—wailing and loud shouts. Avoiding the main path, she stayed sheltered in the forest until she circled around to Ma Slessor's mission house. Tying the goat at the forest's edge, Imatu ran for the missionary's door.

"Imatu!" cried Janie, flinging herself into the bigger girl's arms.

Imatu looked around the hut quickly. Udo and Janie were there, watching Okot, Annie, and Susie. "Where is Ma?" she asked. "Where is Okin?"

Janie pointed to the main clearing of the village. With her heart racing, Imatu left Ma's house and walked slowly toward the drums and wailing. The villagers were milling around, muttering to one another, gesturing with their hands, watching. But no one seemed to notice or care as Imatu crept closer.

Then she saw Okin standing with others around the edge of the main clearing. She touched his arm. A wide smile lit up his face. "You are safe!" he whispered. "We were so worried when . . . when . . ." the boy jerked his head toward the center of the clearing, ". . . when the warriors brought back prisoners from Akpo."

Imatu craned her neck to see. In the center of the clearing a group of prisoners—maybe a dozen—were chained to several posts. She could see one of Chief Akpo's wives . . . several slave men and women, some holding infants or children . . . a couple of free men and . . . and Inyam, her mother.

Hot tears blurred Imatu's eyes. Her shoulders shook as she cried silently. She had been too late. Her mother had been captured. And now . . . maybe she would die.

Okin awkwardly patted her arm. "Don't give up,"

he said kindly. "Pray . . . pray to Jesus. Ma has been praying all night. She says God gives her strength to fight the evil ways. Look." He pointed to the prisoners.

Imatu wiped her eyes with her hands. Blinking rapidly to hold back the tears, she saw the red-haired missionary in a familiar stance: hands on hips, feet apart, facing Chief Edem and the witch doctor.

"You must let these prisoners go, Chief Edem," she was saying. "Killing them will not bring back your son."

"But the son of a chief must be accompanied to the spirit world," said the chief stubbornly.

"You are full of sadness . . . you have lost your son and heir," Ma said, her voice full of sympathy. "But killing these men and women will not make you glad. It will only bring more sadness and grief to the families of Akpo."

"A chief's son must be buried with honor!" interrupted the witch doctor.

"Yes . . . yes, you are right. We must honor him," Mary Slessor agreed, "but not by killing." She stood her ground thoughtfully for a few minutes, then suddenly went running back to the mission house, taking several village men with her. They returned a short while later carrying one of Mary's armchairs, a large umbrella, and an armload of fine cloth and a suit of clothes.

"I was making these clothes for *you*, noble Chief Edem," Ma Slessor explained. "But now we will use them to honor your son." The chief stared after her, perplexed and curious, as she disappeared into the women's yard where the dead boy's mother was moaning over her son.

An hour later, the gate to the yard was swung open, and the villagers were invited to look into one of the huts. Mouths dropped open and eyes popped at the amazing sight before them. The corpse was sitting regally in the armchair, dressed in a brightly colored shirt, an ornamented vest, and loose trousers, over which went a flowing robe, similar to the ones Chief Edem had admired on the Calabar chiefs in King Eyo Honesty's court. The dead boy's hair had been shaved into intricate patterns, painted yellow, then covered with a silk turban. On top of the turban sat a tall black and red hat with plumes of brightly colored feathers.

A whip and a silver-headed stick had been tied to the young man's hands—symbols of his position as heir to the chief. Beside him stood a small table on which had been placed the treasures of the chief's house: jewelry, a comb made from bone, decorated dishes, a skull taken in war, several candles. As a crowning touch, an enormous English umbrella was propped open behind the dead boy's head.

The villagers were delighted at the spectacle and immediately began to chant and dance about. To Ma Slessor's dismay, casks of gin were rolled out, and a long afternoon of drinking added to the merriment and mayhem. But she kept quiet. "Strong drink is a fight for another day," Ma muttered to Okin and Imatu. "Today we fight for the lives of the prisoners."

As the celebration moved into the evening with no sign of letting up, Imatu finally worked up the courage to walk past the guards and creep close to her mother, who sat unmoving among the other prisoners. "Mem?" she whispered. "See? I have water for you."

Inyam looked up dully, took the gourd and drank, then let her head and shoulders sag once more, staring at the ground. Imatu sat silently with her mother as the long evening dragged on, her eyes getting heavier and heavier. . . .

"Wake up, Imatu!" said Ma Slessor, shaking the girl gently. Imatu sat up with a start. She had fallen asleep, her head on her mother's lap.

The village was quiet once more, and most of the villagers had fallen into a drunken sleep in their huts. But as Imatu scrambled to her feet, she realized the guards were unlocking some of the chains and prodding the prisoners to get up.

Her heart lurched with hope. Were they being released? But Ma Slessor shook her head. "The prisoners are being moved into the women's yard where it is more secure," she said. "But nothing will happen tonight. You must go back to the mission house and help Okin take care of the little ones . . . and get some sleep yourself."

"Are you coming, Ma?" Imatu said, watching as a guard pulled Inyam to her feet and prodded her into the women's yard along with the others.

Mary Slessor shook her head. "No . . . I will stay with your mother and the other prisoners. Someone needs to keep watch."

Chapter 9

Baby in the Bush

I MATU WAS WAKENED the next morning by the frantic bleatings of the goat. Uh-oh. She had forgotten the goat, left tied at the edge of the forest and unmilked the night before. Quickly she brought the goat close to the mission house and milked its swollen bag. The other children were beginning to awaken, so she and Okin prepared a breakfast of cold rice and goat's milk, sweetened with sugarcane.

As soon as she could get away, Imatu hurried back to the women's yard. She found Ma Eme trying to persuade Ma Slessor to go back to her house and get some sleep.

"Ah, here is Imatu," said Ma Slessor gratefully. "Yes, if Imatu will keep watch, I will sleep awhile."

"Do not worry," grunted Ma Eme in her crusty way. "I will send the girl to get you if anything happens."

Imatu wasn't sure she could trust Ma Eme. Ma Slessor counted her as a friend, but Ma Eme *was* the sister of Chief Edem and Etim's natural aunt. Whose side was she on, anyway? The girl decided to keep her own eyes and ears open.

Imatu tried to avoid looking through the hut door at the body of Etim, sitting stiffly in the chair, dressed in the fancy clothes. The situation was so weird: a group of moaning prisoners, chained together on one side of the yard, while a dead body in fancy dress sat in the hut on the other. And all around, the women who lived in the yard went about their morning chores: making their fires, grinding cornmeal, feeding their children.

Imatu shivered. What was it like to be dead? Ma Slessor said that when a Christian dies, that person's spirit goes to a happy place called heaven to live with Jesus for ever and ever. But the Okoyong people were afraid of the spirit world. Funerals were frantic rites designed to pacify the angry spirits . . . so unlike the peaceful little funeral for baby Susie's unfortunate twin.

Imatu's thoughts were interrupted as one of the prisoner's mumbled, "Water . . . please, water." She jumped up and ran to one of the village water jars that caught the rain. Back and forth she went several times, bringing gourds full of water for the thirsty prisoners.

But on one of her trips to the water jar, Imatu stopped short. There on a grinding stone sat a handful of black beans. Imatu looked closer and her mouth went dry. Those were not ordinary beans. They were the dreaded *eséré* beans.

Poison beans.

Dropping the gourd of water, Imatu ran to the mission house and burst in the door. "The poison beans . . . I saw the poison beans!" she cried, shaking the sleeping missionary.

Immediately Ma Slessor got up and followed Imatu back to the women's yard. Taking one look at the grinding stone, Ma scooped up the beans and marched to the chief's house.

"You were very pleased with the way we honored your son last night, Chief Edem," she said, eyes blazing. "Why are you planning to still give the trial by poison to the prisoners?"

"Ma . . . Ma," soothed the chief. "Do not be worried. As you know, only the prisoners who are guilty will die from the poison . . . the rest will go free!"

"Nonsense," said Ma Slessor, her voice shaking. "Poison is poison—it can kill innocent people. Would you be willing to drink the poison bean, Chief?"

The chief's eyes narrowed. "Do not insult me, Ma. We are talking about the murder of my *son*. I would not murder my own son."

"It was not murder . . . it was an accident," Ma Slessor insisted. "But if you force the prisoners to take the poison bean ordeal, then you *will* be guilty of murdering innocent people. And," the red-haired woman tilted up her chin defiantly, "you will have to give it to me first."

With that, Ma Slessor turned on her heel and walked away. Sitting down in the gate to the women's yard, she only let the women and children in and out—no one else.

Chief Edem's head wife, Etim's mother, was furious. "If we give the trial by poison," she screeched at Ma Slessor, "it will all be over and we can bury my son. But if you stand in the way, the body will soon stink! His spirit will wander alone in the spirit world! And," she said, shaking her finger in Ma's face, "who will feed all these prisoners? Soon they will die of starvation, eh?"

Ma did not answer. But when the angry woman stalked away, Ma called to Imatu, who was sitting with her mother. "Etim's mother is right about the prisoners," she said quietly. "We must feed them or they will die of hunger. But where are we to get food for so many?"

"Maybe . . . maybe there is food at Akpo," Imatu said. "My mother harvested beans from her garden . . . and yams could still be dug out of the ground."

Ma Slessor's face lit up. "A great idea, Imatu! But you will have to go alone. I need Okin to take care of the children so I can stay with the prisoners . . . and none of the villagers will help you. I hate to ask you to make the trip once more . . . but will you go? Maybe you could take Udo with you. He is big enough to help carry some food."

Imatu nodded. Of course she would go. Wasn't her mother a prisoner? Didn't Inyam sit there as if her life was already gone? Imatu was glad to do something . . . anything except sit and wait, sit and wait.

Within a half hour Imatu and Udo were walking swiftly along the path to Akpo, each carrying long strips of cloth for carrying back whatever food they could find. At least it was daytime and the forest held fewer fears and threats, Imatu thought.

They walked without speaking. But when they had gone about two miles down the path, Udo called out, "Hush! What was that?"

Imatu kept walking. She did not hear anything.

"Wait!" Udo called again. "I hear a baby crying!"

A baby? Imatu stopped and listened. Again she did not hear anything.

"You are imagining things," she snapped at Udo. "We must keep walking. This is not a game we are playing." Besides, she wanted to get out of there. She did not like it when the forest made strange sounds.

They walked the remaining three miles to Akpo, keeping up a quick pace. As they came out of the forest into the clearing, Imatu thought she saw someone—or something—run into the forest on the other side of the burned-out village. She stopped so suddenly that Udo bumped into her.

"Shh," she hissed. They stood still in the shadows at the edge of the forest, scanning all sides of the clearing. Nothing moved.

Finally Imatu ventured out into the clearing with

Udo close on her heels. Still nothing moved. She went first to her mother's hut and stepped into the charred remains. A big lump formed in her throat. Everything her mother had worked so hard for . . . gone.

The girl shook her head as if to get rid of the sad thoughts. She must find food . . . that was all she must think about.

The mud walls of the hut were still standing, open to the sky and breezes above. The palm-thatch roof lay in ashes inside. With a stick she poked among the charred baskets, blankets, and three-legged stools. Then suddenly the stick hit something that made a metallic *ping*. She peered closer. It was the metal pot her mother had brought back from the Creek Town market! Imatu snatched off the lid. It was full of beans.

Three hours later, Imatu and Udo were trudging along the path back to Ekenge. Between them they were carrying a bag of rice found in one of the partly burned huts, Inyam's beans, and dozens of yams dug out of the ground, wrapped in the long cloths they had brought with them and tied on their backs.

When they reached the halfway point, Imatu stopped to rest. The food was heavy and both children were breathing hard. But when they started walking again, Imatu noticed that Udo seemed to be listening for something. She walked faster, forcing him to trot to keep up.

"Wait, Imatu!" the boy called out. "There it is again. Don't you hear it? A baby is crying!"

Imatu listened. Yes, now she heard a noise . . . a faint whimpering, somewhere out in the bush. But it could be anything . . . a panther cub, mewling for its mother . . . a parrot mimicking another animal's cry.

"It's nothing," Imatu said impatiently. "Ma expects us back right away—we mustn't stop for anything. It's already getting dark."

"But—" Udo protested. But Imatu was already out of sight down the path.

The late summer light was fading when Imatu and Udo finally unwrapped their bundles in the mission house yard. Okin had milked the goat and baked some yams in the fire. Imatu drank and ate greedily. Then she stopped. The prisoners must be hungry, too. How could she eat when her mother had had nothing to eat for two days?

Working quickly, Imatu, Okin, and Udo soaked some of the beans to cook the next day, made a pot of rice flavored with peppers and onions and other vegetables, and carried it carefully to the women's yard, where the prisoners were still chained.

Some of the village women looked on, neither hostile nor friendly, as Ma Slessor and the children fed the prisoners. The villagers were simply curious how this strange situation was going to turn out.

Inyam ate hungrily. When the food was gone, she looked at Imatu with sad eyes. "You are a good daughter," she whispered.

Ma Slessor was also pleased. "I knew you could do it," she said proudly, giving both Imatu and Udo a hug. "But I'm glad you got back before dark. I was beginning to get worried."

Udo sighed. "I guess Imatu was right. I heard a baby crying in the bush, but Imatu said we mustn't—"

"What?" hissed Ma Slessor, grabbing both Udo and Imatu and jerking them away from the others. "A baby? What are you talking about? Shh—don't let anyone hear . . . but tell me—*now*."

"B-but it was probably nothing," Imatu stammered, trying to whisper. "Just an animal or . . . or something. I thought I heard the same sound when I ran to Akpo to warn the village . . . but it was nothing."

"But it sounded like a baby," insisted Udo.

"Don't be silly, Udo," said Imatu crossly. "A baby couldn't live that long in the bush."

Ma Slessor ignored her. "Where?" she demanded in a fierce whisper.

Udo tried to explain where he had heard the sound along the trail.

Ma Slessor paced back and forth in the women's yard. Then she sent Udo back to the mission house and took Imatu and Okin outside the women's yard.

"You must both stay here with the prisoners. Don't leave, even for a minute, and don't tell anyone that I am gone. They will think that I have simply gone back to the mission house to sleep. In fact, I will probably be back before anyone even misses me."

"B-but where are you going?" Imatu said.

"Where? To find that baby, of course!" said Ma Slessor. And the next moment she disappeared into the thick darkness.

Chapter 10

Trial by Poison

IMATU LOOKED AROUND FEARFULLY. What would happen if Chief Edem or the witch doctor discovered that Ma Slessor was gone? Most of the prisoners, their stomachs full of rice, had fallen asleep in their chains. But Imatu couldn't sleep. Her whole body was tense.

Outside the women's yard in the central clearing of the village, the witch doctor was building a bonfire. Many of the villagers, both men and women, began gathering around. Chief Edem opened some casks of gin, and the

people began drinking and dancing slowly around the fire.

The fire leaped up taller than a man. The flickering light and weaving figures cast strange shadows. Inside the women's yard, Okin and Imatu looked at each other anxiously. The shadows looked like spirits, Imatu thought, darting through the fence and out again . . . in and out.

Someone looked in the gate of the women's yard, then disappeared. Man or woman . . . Imatu couldn't tell. But shortly after that, the commotion around the fire seemed to get louder.

Why was Ma taking so long? Imatu thought angrily. She should be here, protecting the prisoners, not out searching the darkness for some . . . some abandoned, half-dead baby. If it even was a baby. Maybe the "crying" in the forest was just a sick animal. What if something happened to Imatu's mother because Ma Slessor was out hunting for . . . nothing at all?

Okin interrupted her angry thoughts with a poke on the arm. Imatu looked up . . . into the face of the witch doctor. His eyes darted this way and that. "Where is the white woman?" he demanded.

Imatu's tongue seemed to stick in her mouth. But Okin piped up, "She went to get something and will be back any minute."

The witch doctor grunted, then disappeared as abruptly as he had come. But now Imatu was really frightened. *Please, please, Jesus God,* she found herself praying, *bring Ma Slessor back quickly.* The minutes seemed to drag by, as if time had slowed to the crawl of an insect.

Suddenly several warriors with torches burst into the women's yard, pushed Imatu and Okin aside, and began to unlock the long chain fastening the prisoners together. With their torches they peered into the faces of the now-terrified prisoners until they came to Imatu's mother. Then they pulled Inyam to her feet and pushed her out of the yard toward the fire.

"No, no!" screamed Imatu. "Don't take my mother!" She ran after the warriors but was stopped by the large bulk of Ma Eme, who stepped in her way.

"Hush, girl," said Ma Eme bluntly, holding Imatu by both arms. "You will only make things worse for your mother. You can't do anything to help her now."

Imatu squirmed in Ma Eme's grasp until she could see what was happening around the bonfire. A warrior had forced Inyam to kneel in front of the witch doctor, who was holding a bowl of liquid out in front of him. The drunken shouts and mutterings of the crowd suddenly quieted.

"The murder of young Etim must be avenged!" cried the witch doctor. "His spirit cannot rest until the person who put a curse on him is found. The trial by poison will discover who is guilty . . . and who must die!"

"No-o-o!" screamed Imatu, struggling in Ma Eme's arms. She saw the bowl being held to her mother's lips . . . the fire and the witch doctor and the gawking

crowd seemed to spin around and Imatu thought she was going to faint . . . when a loud shout broke the uneasy silence.

"*STOP!*"

A slight woman's figure in long skirts and bare feet strode quickly through the crowd and knocked the bowl out of the startled witch doctor's hands. Then Ma Slessor immediately whirled toward the crowd of villagers and held out a small bundle she was carrying, wrapped in what looked like Ma's petticoat.

"Look! Look what I have found . . . a baby which has survived several days and nights lying alone in the bush. A miracle baby! Only God the heavenly Father could have kept the leopard and the snakes away and protected this child. See? . . . See?" Ma Slessor walked around the crowd, holding out the tiny child for the villagers to see. The women especially craned their necks and made clicking noises of amazement.

Inyam and the trial by poison had been momentarily forgotten.

Chief Edem, however, quickly tried to regain control of the situation. "Ma . . . Ma Slessor," he said angrily. "You must not keep interfering. We cannot delay—"

"Interfering?" Ma Slessor looked shocked. "I am trying to keep you from doing something you will deeply regret. See this baby?" And she held out the infant toward the chief. "It is a sign! *A sign of life!* God has protected this baby, alone and helpless in the forest, to show us that human life is precious. Saving life—not taking it—is what God wants us to do."

Some of the villagers nodded their heads and murmured to each other. But the witch doctor pointed an accusing finger at the baby Ma Slessor held in her arms. "Why was the child left in the forest?" he sneered. "It must be a monster child . . . a twin . . . fathered by an evil spirit. If you allow it to live, this village will be cursed!"

To Imatu's surprise, Ma Slessor burst out laughing. "The people of this village know better than that," she said, scoffing. "We already have two twin children living among us—baby Susie, the slave woman's child, and my own sweet Janie—and no one who takes care of them has been harmed in any way. The twin taboo is a big lie."

The villagers immediately began arguing and gesturing among themselves, some siding with the witch doctor and others agreeing with Ma Slessor, who continued to show off the tiny infant to each curious person. In the hubbub, Ma Eme let go of Imatu and nodded toward Inyam. Immediately Imatu was beside her mother, helping her stand.

Chief Edem gave a sigh of resignation. "Take the prisoner back to the women's yard," he told one of the warriors. "We will *palaver* tomorrow."

Imatu watched as Janie and Okin and Udo and Okot fussed over the new baby—a girl. Even little

Annie toddled about clapping her hands and saying, "Baby!" She was a tiny thing, with a pinched face and scrawny body from days without food. Ants and insects had bitten her nose and mouth and ears. But everyone shook their heads in amazement and agreed: It was a miracle that the baby was still alive.

Imatu felt confused by all the mixed-up feelings she had inside. She was grateful that Ma Slessor had saved her mother's life from the trial by poison . . . but she was angry that Ma had left the prisoners alone in the first place. What if she had arrived one minute later? It was too close . . . much too close.

And Imatu was glad Ma said that the baby she found in the bush was a sign of life . . . but going to find the baby had almost cost Inyam *her* life.

Imatu also felt guilty that she had ignored the baby's cries when she and Udo heard it on the path. And even though Ma Slessor had not said so, Imatu wondered if the red-haired missionary was mad at her.

Still, she resented all the attention the baby was getting. Didn't everyone realize that Inyam was still in chains, her body and clothes dirty and smelly from three days without being able to wash?

When the morning rain had stopped, Ma Slessor marched over to the village clearing with the new baby, followed by Janie and Okin carrying Susie and Annie, with Okot, Udo, and Imatu bringing up the rear.

"Chief Edem!" she announced pleasantly. "I am ready to *palaver*."

The witch doctor was noticeably absent. He had been deeply offended the night before and had gone away, taking his charms with him. No one seemed too upset. Most of the villagers considered it an honor to have Ma Slessor living among them, and if it was a choice between her and the witch doctor . . . well.

The chief sat on his leather and bamboo stool and rubbed his chin. "The headmen and I have been talking, Ma," he said thoughtfully. "We'll agree to release the prisoners if that will make you happy—"

"Yes, that would make me very happy, Chief Edem," said Ma Slessor with a big smile.

The chief held up his hand. "I am not finished. All the prisoners . . . except for two: the wife of Chief Akpo and my kinswoman, Inyam."

For a moment hope had flickered in Imatu's heart, but it died again.

"But why?" cried Ma Slessor. "Why not release them all?"

"I am trying to be patient, Ma!" said the chief gruffly. "I have listened to you! We will release ten prisoners—isn't that enough?"

Ma started to protest, but the chief held up his hand to silence her. "I will tell you why. Chief Akpo—he ran away, did he not? Doesn't that suggest that he is guilty of putting a curse on my son? Wasn't he angry that you wouldn't let him take weapons to Creek Town? He probably wanted revenge."

"Then why punish his wife?" argued Ma Slessor. "She is innocent . . . let her go."

The chief was silent. Ma Slessor always outtalked him, ruining his good arguments. Finally he said, "All right, I will make a deal. I will let the woman go, but only on one condition: If Chief Akpo is captured, he must face trial to see whether he is innocent or guilty of cursing my son."

"Agreed!" said Ma Slessor happily. Imatu knew that the chief was probably thinking of trial by poison . . . but Ma was thinking of the "talking" kind of trial, where witnesses presented evidence and a judge—usually Ma—decided the verdict.

"What about Inyam?" Ma Slessor pressed.

The chief stuck out his chin stubbornly. "Enough! Be content that only one prisoner stays. Now go away. My heart is grieving for my son." And the chief picked up his stool and went into his hut.

Before the chief could change his mind, Ma Slessor motioned for the guards to unlock the prisoners' chains. "Go quickly," she said to the men and women, who stood up shakily, rubbing their sore wrists and ankles. "Go to the mission house. We will give you each some food to take with you. Now go . . . go."

Only Inyam remained chained to the post in the women's yard.

It was too much for Imatu. She fell on the ground, beating her fists in the dirt and weeping. Inyam just looked away.

Okin knelt down beside his friend. "Don't cry, Imatu," he said anxiously. "Don't cry. There is still hope. See how many prayers Jesus has answered? He can answer one more. . . . Please don't cry."

✧ ✧ ✧ ✧

Imatu stayed beside her despondent mother the rest of the day, leaving only to get her water or food. Everyone left them alone . . . even the guards left.

That evening, the chief, his head wife, and several of the headmen of the village came to sit with the body of the dead boy, still dressed in his fancy clothes, sitting under the large umbrella.

Finally the chief stood up. "We cannot wait any longer," he said. "We must bury the boy tomorrow. *All* will be done tomorrow."

And he walked out of the yard with the others following behind him, without giving Inyam a glance.

"That is a good sign," said Ma Slessor. "Nothing will happen tonight. He made no threats . . . . Whatever is going to happen won't happen until tomorrow. I think we should all get a good sleep."

But Imatu refused to leave her mother. Together they curled up on the ground as the night sank into an inky darkness, the moon and stars hidden by the ever-present clouds of the rainy season.

Sometime in the middle of the night, Imatu thought she heard something. Without moving her position, she opened her eyes but could see nothing. By her mother's deep breathing, she knew Inyam was still asleep.

There—she heard it again . . . as if someone was stealthily moving in the women's yard. Imatu's heart started beating faster, but she was too frightened to move.

Out of the corner of her eye Imatu saw a large, dark shape bend slowly over her mother. She heard a small metal click . . . then another. And then the shape was gone.

Chapter 11

No More Vengeance

IMATU HELD HER BREATH. There was no more movement in the yard. Slowly, carefully, she sat up, peering into the darkness. Who was it? What had he—or she—been doing?

Standing up, she crept quietly to where the shape had stood beside her mother, and she bent down as she had seen the shape bend down. Reaching out her hands she felt the iron chains that bound her mother's wrists and ankles.

They were unlocked. Imatu wanted to shout! . . . but she swallowed the urge and gently shook her mother's arm. Inyam started, but Imatu pressed her hand against her mother's mouth and hissed, "Shh." With deft fingers, she wiggled the unlocked chains off her mother's wrists and ankles and helped her stand. Then, clinging to each other, trembling with the desire to run, mother and daughter stealthily opened the gate to the women's yard.

Five minutes later, Imatu knocked softly on the door of the mission house. "Ma! Ma!" she called in a low voice. "Let us in . . . quickly!"

They heard noises rustling inside, and then the door opened. "Praise to the Lord in heaven!" exclaimed Ma Slessor, clad only in her nightdress, as she pulled them inside.

When the door closed behind her, Inyam sank to the mud floor and began shaking and crying with relief. Even Imatu's knees felt wobbly.

"What . . . how . . .?" Ma said in amazement, looking from one to the other.

Imatu told about the dark shape coming into the yard, then finding the chains had been unlocked. A slow smile spread over Ma Slessor's face. "I think Ma Eme may have been our angel tonight," she said. "But we must never mention our suspicions to anyone else."

Dawn was just beginning to lighten the sky when Imatu heard a shout outside the mission house.

119

"Ma Slessor! Where is the prisoner!"

It was Chief Edem's voice.

Ma Slessor quickly pulled on her skirt and a shawl, and stepped outside.

"The woman Inyam is in my house, Chief," Imatu heard her say pleasantly. "But as you yourself have declared, my house is a house of refuge, and she is safe here."

Imatu heard other voices and murmurings that she couldn't make out. Then the chief said, "It is time to bury my son. Will you and your household join the procession?"

"Of course," Ma Slessor agreed. "Give us a little time to get ready."

Ma Slessor quickly woke the older children, fed them some fruit and cold corn bread, then washed and dressed them in their best clothes. "Imatu, will you watch the three little ones while we are gone?" Ma asked. Imatu nodded gratefully. She knew Ma was giving her an excuse to stay with her mother and not attend the funeral.

As Ma Slessor and her brood started to leave for Etim's funeral, the new baby—who had been named Mary—began to cry in her weak little voice. Immediately Inyam picked her up from the padded box where the baby had been sleeping and began to pat and soothe her.

Ma looked pleased. "You are not afraid of the twin curse, Inyam?" she asked.

Inyam shrugged. "This child is not a twin. Three days before . . . before the warriors came to Akpo, a woman died in childbirth. Her husband did not want to care for it, so the child was thrown away in the bush."

Ma stared at Inyam, opened her mouth as if to say something, then thought better of it and hurried the children out the door. Imatu knew Ma was shocked and angry that a baby could be thrown away like that.

As Imatu fed baby Susie and played with the mischievous Annie, she felt ashamed of how angry she'd felt when Ma ran off to rescue the baby in the bush. To Ma Slessor, every human life was worth fighting for—whether it was an abandoned baby, or a slave, or . . . or a powerless widow like Inyam, or even crusty old Chief Edem.

When Ma Slessor and the children returned several hours later, Inyam had stripped off her smelly garment, washed all over with water and Ma's soap, and put on one of the dresses from the "mission box" from Scotland. Janie ran over to the shy woman, wrapped her arms around Inyam's waist, and looked up into her face. "You are *beautiful!*" she said, her eyes wide.

Everyone laughed.

Okin couldn't wait to tell all the details about the funeral. He described the villagers dressed in their finest clothes and jewelry and hats and feathers, the flute and drum music, and the long procession that wound into the forest to the burial place. "But," said Okin, his eyes dancing, "there were no prisoners to kill to send along with Etim on his journey to the spirit world . . . so they killed a cow instead and put it in his grave!" And the boy rolled on the mud floor, holding his sides as he laughed.

"Stop it now, Okin," chided Ma Slessor. "We mustn't make fun. The old customs and superstitions die hard; at least the cow was a step in the right direction by saving a human life. And Chief Edem seems resigned to the fact that Inyam has taken refuge here."

"Well, if you ask me," said Okin, folding his arms knowingly, "Chief Edem wanted Inyam to escape. That way he could say he didn't give in to all Ma's demands, but Ma would be happy and leave him alone now because Inyam is safe. Why else did he take away the guard and announce to everyone that the funeral would be 'tomorrow'?—to give someone time to help Inyam escape."

Ma Slessor chuckled. "You may be right, Okin . . . but that'll be our secret, all right?"

Inyam waited until Ma Slessor had sung lullabies to the little ones and kissed them good-night. Then she came and sat down beside the missionary.

"Ma . . . you have been a good friend to me," said Inyam. "Thank you for saving my life and giving me refuge in your house. But . . ." Inyam stopped and wrung her hands nervously.

"But?" said Ma Slessor gently.

"I have been inside the mission house for three

weeks! I dare not go outside—I am still an escaped prisoner and could be captured again. But . . . but I can't stay cooped up here forever. I must go away . . . far away!"

Imatu looked up from the cooking pots she and Okin were scrubbing by the fireplace. She liked staying at the mission house with Ma Slessor and Okin and Janie and the other children. She didn't want to leave . . . besides, where would they go? The village of Akpo was just a pile of ashes.

Ma Slessor echoed Imatu's thoughts. "But where would you go, Inyam? Maybe I should talk to Chief Edem—"

"No! No," said Inyam, shaking her head vigorously. "I don't want to live in Ekenge, even if Chief Edem said yes—which he won't. I—I'll go find my sister and her husband . . . the people of Akpo are hiding *somewhere* in the valley."

Ma Slessor frowned. "Yes . . . but I worry about your safety in the forest alone. And what about Imatu?"

Inyam looked at her daughter, who was staring anxiously back at her.

"She is safe here with you . . . if you will let her stay," said Inyam finally. "And I know she is eager to attend Reading School again. I will leave the goat to help pay for her food. Maybe later, when I find a place to live . . ." Her voice trailed off.

"Of course she can stay. She is a big help to me," said Ma Slessor. "But let's talk about it more in the morning. We can make some plans. We'll begin asking around the area if anyone knows where the Akpo refugees are."

But the next morning, when Imatu heard the goat bleating, begging to be milked, her mother was gone.

The rainy season ended early in October and the dry season began. Three months . . . four months . . . five months passed, and Imatu heard nothing from her mother. A few times she and Okin walked the trail to Akpo, to see if anyone had returned. But the walls of the roofless mud huts were crumbling, and weeds and grasses crowded the abandoned garden plots.

Then one day in early March, Ma Slessor came back full of news from a visit to villages farther north. "As I was walking back along the trail," she said to Ma Eme, who had been staying at the mission house in her absence, "I passed a small group of huts hidden in the forest. I thought I heard someone call my name . . . and then suddenly a familiar face peered through the bushes. Who do you think it was?"

Imatu's eyes widened. "Not . . . my mother?"

Ma Slessor laughed. "Yes! It was Inyam! And her sister's family . . ." Then Ma's smile faded. "But she did not look like the beautiful Inyam who left here six months ago. She is thin and dirty . . . life in the forest is very hard. Chief Akpo was there, too—but

he has been ill. He is afraid to come home, because Chief Edem insisted he would have to face trial."

Ma Eme lifted her bulk off the mud "couch," and started out the door.

"Where are you going?" asked Ma Slessor in surprise.

The big woman beckoned. "Come. Bring all the children. I think it is time you talked to my brother."

They made a strange procession: Ma Eme moving like a steamship through the village with Ma Slessor and all her children trotting to keep up right behind her. Chief Edem, sitting in front of his hut, smoking a clay pipe, looked up in surprise as Ma Eme and her entourage came to a stop in front of him.

"Ma Slessor! I heard you had returned from your visit north. I am glad to see you well," said the chief.

For a few minutes the missionary made small talk with the chief until Ma Eme cleared her throat impatiently.

"Chief Edem, it has been six months since you buried your son," said Mary Slessor. "Don't you think it is time to bury old grievances as well? Five miles from here a once-thriving village sits abandoned and broken. Old friends and neighbors are living like wild animals in the forest because they are afraid to come home. It is our loss as well as theirs."

Chief Edem puffed on his pipe and looked at the red-haired woman thoughtfully.

"God's Book says that anyone can love his friends—that's easy," Ma Slessor continued. "But it takes a truly great person to love his enemies."

Chief Edem continued to puff on his pipe. Finally he took it out of his mouth. "Very well, Ma. You can tell Chief Akpo that all thought of vengeance is gone from my heart, and if he wishes to return to his own village or live in your home or go anywhere among the Okoyong, he is at liberty to do so."

"And Inyam? And the other people who were chased away from Akpo?"

Chief Edem gestured with his pipe. "All can come home. I give my word, no harm will come to them."

Imatu could hardly believe her ears!

But it was a bittersweet homecoming. Ma Slessor had to go three times to the little huts hidden in the forest to persuade Chief Akpo, Inyam, and the others that it was safe to return. And when they finally did straggle into their old clearing, they were met by the ruins of their once-vigorous village.

That same day, however, the refugees were surprised to see half the village of Ekenge coming out of the forest, carrying bamboo and palm leaves to help rebuild the huts. Mats, blankets, baskets, and cooking pots were donated to help the villagers of Akpo get back on their feet. Chief Edem himself was with them, bringing bags of seeds to plant.

Imatu went back to Ekenge for one more night, to get the goat and say goodbye to Okin and Janie and all the other Slessor children.

"Why are you going away, Imatu?" asked Janie, her eyes brimming with tears. "Don't you like living with us?"

"Oh, yes," said Imatu, blinking back her own tears. "But I must go help my mother plant new crops and . . . and make more baskets to sell in Creek Town."

"We will go see Imatu often," Ma Slessor assured the children. "Maybe we will even start a Reading School in Akpo!"

"The chief of Ifako has finally started to build the church that he promised," Okin spoke up. "When it is finished, everyone from Ekenge and Akpo and Ifako will be invited to worship there."

"Yes! I will come," said Imatu, almost fiercely. "Someday I want to read God's Book for myself." Imatu wanted to see if God's Book really said to love your enemies . . . or if Ma Slessor had just made that up to get Chief Edem to change his mind.

Just then they heard Chief Edem calling Ma Slessor from the mission yard. This was unusual; the chief rarely came to the mission house. Ma went outside to greet him while the children stared from the doorway. The chief was alone in the twilight.

To their surprise, Chief Edem knelt down, his forehead touching the dirt, his hands holding Ma Slessor's feet. "Thank you . . . thank you, Ma," he said humbly. "You have done a brave and wonderful thing. You kept me from killing other people when my son died. You told me to forgive my enemies. I am weary of the old ways . . . the fear and fighting and superstitions . . . which always end in death."

Ma Slessor hardly knew what to say. "Dear friend," she said kindly, helping the chief to his feet, "it is the love of God that has the power to bring life instead of death."

That night as Imatu fell asleep for the last time in the mission house, with Janie cuddled against her, Ma's words tumbled over and over in her mind. *The love of God . . . life instead of death . . . the love of God . . . life instead of death . . .*

Chapter 12

Moving Forward

THE CHURCH SCHOOL IN IFAKO was filled to overflowing with young and old from neighboring villages. Several years had passed since Mary Slessor had first come to live among the Okoyong people in Ekenge; this was Ma's anniversary celebration.

Imatu, now a handsome young woman, sat nervously at the front glancing over the people as they jostled each other for space to sit or stand on the hard mud floor. Ma Eme was there, sitting regally on a wooden box, fanning herself with a colorful paper fan, a treasure from the "mission box." But her brother, Chief Edem, had died of smallpox

during the epidemic that had wiped out half the population of Ekenge and many people from other villages . . . including Imatu's mother, Inyam.

Sitting on the ground in the front row under the watchful eye of Janie, now a young woman herself, were Mary Slessor's family of children: Annie, Alice, Mary, Maggie, Dan, Whitie, and Asequo. Imatu felt a familiar lump in her throat when she thought of baby Susie, who had died at fifteen months after being accidentally burned by a spilled pot of boiling water. As for Udo and Okot, they had returned to their own families in Creek Town after being trained by Ma Slessor for several years.

Imatu could hardly believe Okoyong was the same place she had lived before Ma Slessor had come. So much had changed: There was no more human sacrifice . . . and very little twin murder . . . raiding and plundering of other villages had stopped . . . disputes were settled in tribal court with Ma as judge . . . and trading had improved their lives—raising their standard of living and giving people productive work to do rather than wasting time drinking and fighting. . . .

The talking and shuffling died as Mary Slessor stood up to welcome everyone. Though she was wearing her "best" dress from the mission box, Ma was still hatless and barefooted, as were her black sisters sprinkled throughout this amazing congregation— the first of its kind among the Okoyong people. Imatu realized that the red hair had deepened to a dark brown, and the missionary's skin was like weathered parchment.

"Dear brothers and sisters," Ma Slessor began in the Efik language, "I am deeply moved to be here with you today. Today is a special day . . . the happiest day since I came to live among you . . . because today we are going to baptize seven young men and women who are dedicating their lives to the one true God."

Imatu flushed and glanced nervously at the other six "young men and women" sitting on either side of her. The young men had white shirts on, and the young women wore colorful blue dresses that Ma had sewn herself.

Okin, who was sitting beside Imatu, gave her a little grin. "Relax, Imatu," he whispered, "or I will have to pinch you, and won't *that* cause a scene!"

Imatu stifled a giggle. Her childhood friend still knew how to make her laugh.

"This is also a special day," Ma was continuing, "because our guest today is Reverend W. T. Weir, who has come from Creek Town to conduct the baptism, and to receive these new converts as the first members of the Okoyong Christian Church!"

Ma sat down, beaming, as the packed church clapped enthusiastically. A spontaneous song started, and for ten minutes the thatched roof shook with a joyful noise. But the singing and clapping died to a rustle as Reverend Weir—a serious-looking white man—took his place before them.

He got right to the point. "Will the candidates for baptism please stand?" he said in Efik.

Imatu, Okin, and the others stood up.

"Okin, will you come forward and kneel?" said the missionary.

Okin knelt in front of Reverend Weir.

"Do you confess your faith in Jesus Christ, the Son of God, as your Savior and Lord?" the man asked.

Okin nodded. "I do, gladly," he said in a strong voice.

Imatu saw that Ma Slessor was blowing her nose in a handkerchief.

"Do you confess your sins and accept the forgiveness Christ offers by His death on the cross?"

Again Okin said, "I do."

Reverend Weir lifted a pitcher of water. "Then I baptize you in the name of the Father, the Son, and the Holy Ghost." And he poured water—lots of water—over Okin's head. It ran down the young man's face and shoulders, soaking his white shirt, and his smile glistened with happiness.

Imatu was watching Okin so intently that she was startled when someone poked her and whispered, "He called your name."

Imatu's knees shook as she walked a few paces and knelt in front of the missionary from Creek Town. The man asked her the same questions he had asked Okin. She wanted so much to answer strongly and clearly from her heart, but her voice seemed to squeak in her own ears. Then she felt the water pouring over her head and shoulders . . . and suddenly Imatu felt as if she might burst from happiness. All the pain and anger and fear of the old ways seemed to wash away. And she knew it was true: The love of God had the power to bring life instead of death.

Warm tears of happiness mingled with the cold water dripping from her head as Imatu got to her feet and stood beside Okin. One by one the other five young men and women were baptized and pronounced members of the first Christian church in Okoyong.

But the celebration wasn't over yet. Because Reverend Weir was an ordained minister, Ma had asked him to serve the Lord's Supper to all the Christians in the house—including Imatu and the others who had just been baptized. Imatu took the small bit of flat bread and sip of wine, which symbolized the broken body and spilled blood of Christ. "Eat and drink this together in remembrance of Me," Reverend Weir said, repeating Jesus' words to His followers.

"Christians do this all over the world," Ma had explained to Imatu. "Besides reminding us of Jesus' sacrifice in our place, the Lord's Supper also reminds us that we belong to the family of God all over the world!"

As she chewed the bread and swallowed the wine, Imatu thought how wonderful it was to belong to a new family—God's family. She had felt so alone when her mother died of smallpox . . . but Ma and Okin and Janie truly seemed like her family, too. "That's because you too have become a child of the heavenly Father," Ma had smiled when Imatu told her how she felt.

After the Lord's Supper, all the people sang Psalm 103, which Ma had taught them in the Efik language—though the tune was a Scottish melody:

He forgives all my sins
And heals all my diseases.
He keeps me from the grave
And blesses me with love and mercy.

The service had been long, but even the children were quiet and still as their beloved Ma finally stood up and spoke directly to the young men and women who had just been baptized. "What has happened here today is not my doing," she said seriously. "Give God all the glory! I am only His hands and feet. In fact, the people of Okoyong now look to you more than me for proof of the power of the Gospel. Whether I am here or not, the church of Jesus Christ must carry on His work—and you are that church."

Something in her words troubled Imatu. Afterwards, as the people moved outside and set up the feast they had prepared for the occasion, Imatu looked for a chance to speak to Ma Slessor alone. But everyone wanted to shake Ma's hand and greet Reverend Weir and congratulate the newly baptized young people. Only hours later, when the people finally began to drift home to their various villages and Ma was collecting her children, did Imatu see her chance.

"I will walk home with you," she offered. Imatu fell in step with Ma as the Slessor family walked the

trail to the mission house.

"Ma . . . what did you mean when you said,

'Whether I am here or not'?"

Ma did not answer for a few minutes. But finally she said, "I am feeling restless, Imatu. There are still so many villages farther inland that have never heard the Gospel . . . like the Aros people."

Imatu was shocked. "But, Ma! The Aros are cannibals!"

Ma gave a little laugh. "All the more reason they need the Gospel of peace, eh?"

"But, Ma," Imatu protested, "aren't you afraid?"

"Oh, yes," Ma Slessor admitted.

"Then you must have more courage than . . . than even the Okoyong chiefs, who never venture among the Aros if they can help it."

Ma shook her head. "Not courage . . . faith. Faith in our God. What is courage anyway, but faith conquering fear?"

The two women walked silently for a while, watching the children skipping ahead on the trail in the twilight. Then Ma said, "Imatu, when I was a lassie about your age—still in my twenties—a great missionary to Africa died. His name was David Livingstone. In many ways he was my hero . . . I wanted to be like him. I especially remember one thing he said: 'I am ready to go anywhere, provided it be forward.'"

Ma Slessor stopped and turned to Imatu. "It is time for me to move forward . . . time to leave my work here in hands like yours."

"*Me!*" gasped Imatu. "But . . . but . . ."

"Yes, you and Okin and the others. There is so

much you can do! You can teach the Reading School and care for those who need refuge in the mission house and tell the Jesus stories to the little ones . . . oh, there is much you can do."

A funny feeling stirred inside Imatu. Yes . . . yes, she could do those things. Hadn't she been helping Ma for several years now?

"But I could never take your place—no one could," Imatu said quietly, looking at the ground.

"Of course not!" Ma laughed, lifting Imatu's chin with her finger. "You must take your own place . . . while I find the next place God has for me."

Ma looked down the trail. All the children except Asequo, who was snoring gently on Imatu's back, had disappeared.

"Come on," Ma said laughing. "We must catch up or they will all hide and jump out at us and scare us half to death. Cannibals are one thing . . . but mischievous children are an entirely different matter."

And grabbing Imatu by the hand, the two women ran laughing down the trail.

More About Mary Slessor

MARY MITCHELL SLESSOR, a red-haired Scottish "lassie," was born in Aberdeen, Scotland, in 1848. She was the second of seven children, the daughter of a shoemaker. Though her childhood was marked by hardship and hunger because of her alcoholic father, Mary took a keen interest in missions early in life.

Poverty forced the family to move to Dundee when Mary was ten, and the next year she went to work in a weaving mill while still attending school. By age fourteen, she was working full time in a factory to help support the family. Converted at a young age, she was active in her local Presbyterian church, volunteering to teach Sunday school among rowdy street kids.

When Doctor David Livingstone, famous missionary and explorer in Africa (see the Trailblazer book, *Escape from the Slave Traders*), died in 1874, his life and work inspired many—including Mary Slessor. She applied to the Calabar Mission, which had been in Calabar, Africa (what we know today as southern Nigeria), for thirty years. When she was accepted, she made arrangements for the care of her mother and sisters, and sailed in late summer, 1876, for Calabar. She was twenty-seven.

As Mary was waiting to board her ship, the *Ethiopia*, she saw many casks of gin and rum being loaded on board for sale and trade in Africa. She shook her head sadly and said, "Scores of casks and only one missionary."

Mary's first assignment was to the mission station in Duke Town along the Calabar River, under the guidance of veteran missionaries "Daddy" and "Mammy" Anderson. Her basic duties were to teach in the mission school, learn the Efik language, and simply "visit" with the Africans, establishing relationships and learning their beliefs and their ways.

But Mary was essentially a pioneer and impatient to move beyond the well-ordered work of the established mission. When she returned from her first furlough in 1880, she was reassigned and given charge of the work in Old Town, three miles upriver. Uncomfortable with the discrepancies in lifestyle between the European missionaries in Africa and the native peoples, Mary chose to live very simply, eating native food and living in a mud hut African-style—with a few personal touches, such as a real door and windows. This enabled her to send much of her salary back to Scotland in support of her family.

But Mary also realized that much of African life was rooted in pagan customs and beliefs—such as witchcraft, twin-murder, polygamy, buying and selling of slaves, and even cannibalism—that needed to be changed if the ethics of the Gospel were to take effect. One superstition she confronted head on was that the birth of twins was a curse. It was thought that an evil spirit fathered one of the children; usually both twins were murdered or left out in the jungle to die, and the mother of the twins was driven out of the village and shunned (often to die).

When Mary returned to Scotland for her second furlough in 1883, she took along a six-month-old twin she had rescued, whom she named Janie after her youngest sister. (She had failed to save Janie's twin brother.) Janie was the first of several twins who became her own "family" of adopted orphans, while she rescued and cared for many more who were then placed with sympathetic families. After twenty-two years in Calabar, Mary, by her own count, had rescued fifty-one twins from death!

Shortly after returning to Calabar in December, 1885, Mary received word that first her mother, and then her last surviving sister, had died. Though she was grief stricken, she set her face even more resolutely toward the interior of Africa, which had never heard the Gospel; "There is no one now who will be anxious for me if I go," she said.

Her destination was the Okoyong people, who were related to the Bantu race of Central and South Africa. They were a tall, regal people, but addicted to witchcraft and human sacrifice, fighting and warring, thieving and plunder. Nonetheless, noting her courage to come alone, they welcomed the "white Ma" to live among them.

She settled in the village of Ekenge about four miles inland from the Calabar River, also establishing a school and "meetinghouse" in Ifaku village two miles away. She believed that "school and the Gospel" went hand in hand. The people were eager to learn "book," and she insisted that all people, young and old, slave and free, could come to her school. And in every human interaction she never let an opportunity go by to share the Gospel.

With unbelievable courage, in spite of sometimes weakened health and bouts of malaria, Mary—or "Ma" as she was called by everyone—confronted the chiefs and the people in their pagan practices. She stood up for justice in their dealings with one another, and her reputation as a peacemaker soon brought chiefs and people from neighboring villages to seek her counsel and advice. The Okoyong people viewed her as their unofficial magistrate, making judgment between disagreeing parties—or even warring villages. In 1892, the British designated her as the official vice-consul for the area, a position she held for many years; and in 1894 she helped oversee an agreement between the local chiefs and the British consul, Sir Claude Macdonald, at which time the chiefs agreed to quit their "murderous practices" (such as human sacrifice at the death of a chief); in return he declared them a free people.

Mary stayed among the Okoyong people for fifteen years (minus two furloughs). Her accomplishments at the midway point were considerable. Raiding, plundering, and the stealing of slaves had stopped. People were as safe traveling, visiting, and trading among the Okoyong as in Calabar. The people did not want a king (black or white), but they did ask Ma to serve as consul in their tribal court. When she had arrived, the only trade had been guns, gin, and chains, but Mary encouraged the people to increase their agricultural efforts in palm and peanut oil, yams, cassava root, rubber, etc.—not only to raise their standard of living but to use their idle hours more productively as one way to decrease wanton drinking and fighting. Human sacrifice at funerals and to avenge sickness or accidents had ceased; twin-murder had decreased, and in general there was a new regard for human life.

After her third furlough, Mary moved her mission headquarters to Akpap, a market village farther inland. Finally in 1902, after fifteen years among the Okoyong people, the first communion service was held and eleven young people were baptized. Seven of those eleven were her own adopted children: Annie, Alice, Mary, Maggie, Dan, Whitie, and Asequo.

But Mary was restless. There were still tribes who had never heard the Gospel of Jesus Christ! And

Mary was at heart a pioneer. Others could take over the church she had established; she must push on. She was due for another furlough in 1904; instead, Mary spent her own time and her own money to search out a new mission base in order to reach the fierce Aros and Ibibios tribes along Enyong Creek, who had long been dominated by "The Long Juju," a mysterious and powerful witchcraft.

She finally settled on the village of Itu at the junction of the Cross River and Enyong Creek as a mission base. Because of its strategic position, Itu had formerly been a slave market; under Mary's supervision, a medical center was established there, which was eventually named the Mary Slessor Hospital. Several years later, in 1913, she was awarded the title Honorary Associate of the Order of St. John of Jerusalem (an order dedicated to the relief of the sick and suffering) for establishing the hospital at Itu and other humanitarian work in Calabar.

Even though her health was deteriorating, still Mary pushed on. She alternated between several villages farther north, traveling in a rickshaw-type cart pulled by young boys. Beloved and respected by slaves and chiefs alike, she continued to settle quarrels, nurture unwanted babies, teach men and women and children to read "book," and preach the Gospel of Jesus Christ.

Finally, on January 13, 1915, at the age of sixty-six, she succumbed to fever and dysentery for the last time, with this prayer on her lips: *"O Abasi, sana mi yok"* (O God, release me). But her spirit and influence lived on. As Carol Christian and Gladys Plummer said in concluding *God and One Redhead,* their biography of Mary Slessor:

Yet wherever along the lower reaches of the Cross River, and particularly the Enyong Creek, an African woman earns her own living; wherever a mother of twins rears her children and her husband stands loyally by her; wherever parties to a quarrel seek the mediation of the courts instead of leaping for their machetes, something endures of the spirit of a slight, red-haired woman who in the midst of this region was whirlwind, earthquake, fire, and still small voice.

For Further Reading

Christian, Carol and Gladys Plummer. *God and One Redhead: Mary Slessor of Calabar.* Grand Rapids, Mich.: Zondervan, 1970.

Livingstone, W.P. *Mary Slessor of Calabar: Pioneer Missionary.* London: Hodder and Stoughton, 1915.

Miller, Basil. *Mary Slessor: Heroine of Calabar.* Minneapolis, Minn.: Bethany House Publishers, 1974.